CORNER

CORNER

HAYLEY GABRIELLE

CORNER
© 2019 Hayley Gabrielle

First Edition

Book design by Sue Balcer
Cover art by Valentyna Petyurenko (Jenteva Art)
ISBN: 978-0-6484452-4-1

Visit the author's website at
www.hayleygabrielle.com

For Alex

Contents

Open.. 1

2 7

3 16

4 19

5 28

6 36

7 50

8 52

9 54

10 57

11 67

12 78

13 Jesse 94

14 99

15 104

16 110

17 113

18 Ray 125

19 130

20 133

21 144

22 150

23 154

24 159

25 167

Dot's Journal 170

26 173

27 179

28 *Flo* 188

29 195

30 198

31 205

32 212

33 219

34 225

35 228

36 239

37 248

38 252

39 255

40 257

41 *Darcy* 264

42 272

43 274

44 282

45 310

Closed 293

Acknowledgements 295

About the Author 299

It made my heart race every time, but that wasn't an unusual occurrence for me.

"Hi, how are we all going with our menus?" What, was I having a meal with them too?

"Good evening–" Way too formal.

"Can I get you any drinks?" Yes. The unobtrusive drinks offer. It became my go-to when I started at *Corner*, sweating at the palms and pits and everywhere else.

I was awkward in most things I did. There must have been some wiring missing–the wiring that allows ordinary humans to actually function in ordinary social scenarios.

To me, hell on earth was the walk up to a table of new faces. Old people were intimidating because they always seemed to give you this sympathetic look, like they knew you were quietly dying inside. Young people were intimidating because they looked you up and down, for the same reason. Maybe most of that was in my head, but my head always knew how to insist something was real even when it probably wasn't.

I kept a lot of worry to myself. Mum and Dad were the only people who really knew how fast and hard my brain worked, but even then—I didn't let them in on the full extent of it.

When fear didn't make sense, it was harder to admit. On the occasions I tried, its credibility was often diminished to words like *antisocial* and *dramatic* and *just relax*.

The fact that it was me in the car park that night seemed like a cruel lesson or joke played by some divine entity. Like they were jabbing their finger at me, saying—*you think the world is scary? I'll show you scary.*

All of a sudden, the irrational turned rational. Had I been crazy before? Or was I crazy now?

I had been anxious. Excruciatingly nervous. And now all that was justified.

But I had reason to be a lot of other things, too. There was goodness in what came before, and even what came after. There were people and moments more worthy of my attention. I want to tell you about them, first.

———•———

Coming home felt like shedding a layer of skin that had built up so much my feet were starting to drag from the weight. It was a Tuesday, after a series of painfully lengthy uni lectures, that I shrugged that layer away and just about tumbled inside.

I found Mum chopping veggies in the kitchen, and could tell instantly something was up because of the way her shoulders were when she turned to me with teary, onion eyes. Before broaching a topic she deemed of some significance, those narrow shoulders would always rise right up to her ears.

She was skin and bone, my Mum. It meant she could hardly hide any shift in her posture, however minute.

"Hey Dotty, just wait on a tick," she said before I could make a run for it.

"Mmm?" I hesitated, clutching my laptop bag as though it were a life vest that could take me far, far away before disaster could strike.

"How was your day?" She smiled sweetly, as if this was all she wanted to say. I couldn't be fooled.

"It was all right."

"Uncle Ray called today–" Uh-oh. "Apparently he's a waitress down at the Scarlett Street Corner, had to let her go for stealing. From the bar I believe … a bottle of something. The manager caught her with it. Mustn't be too bright, that girl. They have cameras and everything. What could she expect?"

I shook my head along with the story, still with one foot on the first step up to safety–my room. I could see where this was going and I couldn't let it go there.

"Anyway, he suggested you might want to take up a few shifts?"

My anxiety level skyrocketed but I worked it into a simple, raised brow. I'd become good at controlling external signs of my panic around Mum.

Uncle Ray owned Corner himself, a restaurant chain he'd spent years tirelessly moulding into success. He was Mum's older brother and she knew exactly how to boss him around.

"That's the way it's always been," he'd declare at almost every family dinner. "As kids she'd dress me up and make me play Barbies," he'd say, "and if I refused, she'd run around beating me with the Ken doll until I gave in." We would laugh, because he always put on this traumatized voice to recount it.

I was convinced it wasn't Uncle Ray who proposed I'd be a great help at the restaurant. By anyone's standard, I was hardly the ideal waitress type. My brain was like a chalkboard and most forms of small talk drew nails down it. Even looking someone in the eye for more than a few seconds made me squirm.

Uncle Ray had known me long enough to observe my shyness, at the very least. Mum would've suggested this. There wasn't a doubt in my mind.

"Since Cameron ..." Mum hesitated then, and turned to the pan to give the onion a stir. She knew I hated it when she brought up Cameron. "You're isolating yourself, Dotty. And I just ..." she didn't go on, just let out an agitated puff through her nose.

I sighed, long and heavy. Cameron had been my boyfriend, and a good one, up until he decided to jet off to America for a 'study semester'. We tried to maintain a long distance thing, but it flopped fairly quickly, and he didn't seem to mind all that much.

The worst part was that I had kind of neglected my other friendships while I was with him, and hadn't made any real ones at uni. I wished they'd taught us in high school how to make lasting friends once we were out. Probably would've been more useful than trigonometry, to be honest.

"I'm not isolating myself," I retorted, frowning at her like the notion was inconceivable. But it wasn't. I knew that isolation wasn't exactly healthy, but it was easy. When you had to factor other people into your life, you lost control. And besides, worrying about myself was work enough.

"Regardless," she said with a note of finality that scared me half to death, "he's family, and we need to help him where we can."

"He can hire someone else!" I tried, my panic rising to another level.

But Mum was already shaking her head. "I told him you were almost finished with this semester, and you'd give him a call to talk about your availability."

"*What?*"

"It'll be good for you," she said, confirming my every suspicion that this was a setup. I groaned and charged up the stairs.

It's bizarre looking back now. Simple conversations and fleeting decisions—mostly trivial until hindsight rears its head and the dots connect.

What if Cameron had stayed around? What if that waitress hadn't swiped a bottle? What if Uncle Ray had filled the position before Mum got to him?

If I had to pinpoint my first significant corner, it would be that afternoon in the kitchen. I see every decision I made from then on as a choice between a series of tables. Like each one was set with covered dishes under silver lids and I couldn't see what was coming until it came, what I would be in for, until I took a seat.

2

"Sweetie, I dropped by Ray's today," Dad said from the door of my bedroom. "He asked me to give you this."

I'd barely closed my laptop before he threw a blue cloth at my head. I grabbed at it and held it up–my heart sank. "An apron?"

Dad winked. "You'll look great. The next Betty Crocker, or … that woman … who's that woman who makes the cheesecakes? The ones your Mum freezes?"

"Sara Lee?" I ventured, and couldn't help but grin at him. "I don't think she's the actual chef, Dad."

"Isn't she?" He looked genuinely puzzled. "What, you think it's just the company name?"

I shrugged. "Not sure." It didn't seem an important point to clarify, so I flipped my laptop open again and went back to my Financial Literacy assignment–which unfortunately wasn't much more interesting than the history of Sara Lee. But it was my last assignment for the semester, so I was giving it a red-hot crack.

Kramer slunk through the doorway, his long, grey tail curling around Dad's leg. My parents were Seinfeld fans, hence the name. But this Kramer didn't burst into rooms like the TV character. He was a ragdoll–about seven years old now. They were known to be quiet and placid and always up for a cuddle. I aspired to live my life with the ease of Kramer.

Dad was loitering. "There would've been a Sara Lee originally," he muttered, appearing greatly perturbed by the thought. "I'll have to look it up." We rarely went one day without Dad suggesting we look up something.

Finally he left my doorway and I heard him go to Mum and ask if she knew about Sara Lee.

They were a funny combination, my folks. Like salted caramel–Dad was the sweet and Mum was the salty and even though it was weird when you thought about it, somehow they worked together.

I took a moment to inspect the apron Dad had thrown at me, just as Kramer jumped up onto the bed to sniff at it too. Navy blue, with Corner in white stitching across the front pocket.

Uncle Ray owned three Corner restaurants here in Melbourne, one in Queensland and two in Sydney. I was being forced into one of the former, nearest our place.

Tomorrow was tour day, and already I was dreading it. I'd been before for dinner a few times with Mum and Dad, but apparently Uncle Ray wanted to explain how everything ran before my first shift that weekend.

I tossed the apron aside and pulled Kramer onto my lap. One lingering hope remained—that he would deem me unfit for the job early on and I'd get out of working through the summer. It wouldn't be hard to convince him of my social incompetence. It came fairly naturally to me.

———•———

Corner was close to the city, but not so close that I'd need to stress about parking. Which didn't matter, because there was plenty else to stress about.

My hair was pale brown and so short that when I tied it up, bits of it came loose at my neck. I'd made the cut when Cameron and I broke up as a bit of a *screw you* statement. But soon after I realised it was also possible to perceive it as—*now that you're gone, I'm going to have a Britney breakdown and shave my hair like a smurf*. I couldn't wait for it to grow out.

I tied the Corner apron over black, skinny jeans and a white shirt. Over the phone Uncle Ray had said to wear a collar, but he hadn't specified a colour. So I'd gone with my old school shirt, only now I was thinking white wasn't a clever choice since it was bound to show up spills and other grimy bits and bobs.

I chewed my lip as I made for the entrance. It was a nervous tic. My lips were constantly chapped and papaw ointment was my best friend. I smeared some on, pocketing it with slightly trembling hands before pressing the glass door open.

All the tables but one were empty–it was only five o'clock, so the dinner rush was still a safe distance away.

I cast my gaze around, meeting the eyes of a tall guy with sandy hair polishing cutlery. He dropped his cloth and strode over while I averted my eyes in desperate search of Uncle Ray.

"Hi." The guy stopped before me. His smile was bright, lighting up his whole face in a way that usually only came from knowing someone a long time. "You looking for a … table?" A puzzled frown spread across his brow as his gaze fell to my apron. "Or …"

"I'm here to see my uncle," I quickly interposed, scanning the restaurant again. It was an eclectic mix of wooden chairs around heavy oak tables, vaguely reminiscent of an antique furniture store. There were exposed timber beams set across a high, pitched ceiling, and the lights were warm and hung low. The kitchen was open just enough to reveal a white chef's cap.

I remember Uncle Ray telling us about the interior design–how he wanted it to feel like walking into someone's home. I wasn't sure if it felt like walking into a home or a funky church, but either way he'd done well.

"Oh." The guy looked surprised. "Cool. He's over at the bar—if you just—oh, I'm Darcy by the way."

"Hey," I said lamely. "Dot."

"Sorry?"

Blood rushed into my cheeks. "My name. It's Dot."

"Ohhh." Darcy motioned for me to follow him. "Dot," he murmured as we went. "Is that like, Dorothy?"

"Yeah," I admitted a little sheepishly.

"No shit." He inclined his head as if to consider it, then nodded and smiled to himself. "That's cool."

I always thought my parents cursed me with the name Dorothy. Dot. A dot was an *almost nothing*. A near-invisible speck. And that was either how I felt or how I wanted to feel. I could never quite figure out which.

"Dotty!" My Uncle was behind the bar with another guy around my age in glasses, his hair gelled high. Uncle Ray strode out with open arms. "How are you, girl?"

I tried to smile. "Good thanks."

"Good thanks," Uncle Ray imitated my supposedly robotic monotone, a broad grin showing up in his cropped beard. "Look at you." He gestured to my apron. "Raring to go—I like it."

He was well built for a man in his fifties, with wide shoulders and black hair speckled a frosted grey that only seemed to strengthen his charisma.

Growing up, I was always a little terrified of him for being so consistently sure of himself, but a little in awe of it too. Not only was he loaded from the success of the Corner chain, he'd also survived a messy divorce with Aunty Rhea who turned out to be a complete psycho, and when she left he basically raised my cousin Peter on his own.

Remembering it all now, I was suddenly glad I went. Even if it *was* Mum's wacky idea to force me into interacting with other human life forms, Uncle Ray had spent much of his life without the helping hands he deserved. If I could offer mine now, this might be worth the pain.

As he took me around, his voice boomed from wall to wall. I wondered more than once whether it would disturb the only couple seated, glancing nervously their way every time Uncle Ray laughed or called across the room to that waiter, Darcy. But then, I thought, he acted no differently in his own home whenever we visited, and so his nonchalance almost complimented the chic, homey vibe of the furnishings around us. He was a part of them too.

In the kitchen I was introduced to a bald-headed chef, and Jude—the manager of the restaurant. I'd heard a bit about him over the years. He and Uncle Ray met at the gym, believe it or not. My uncle was a bit of a gym junkie. Dad often teased him for it, but I think that was mostly because of Dad's own pot-belly insecurities.

"My niece, Dorothy," Uncle Ray announced to Jude, and we shook hands. "Or Dot, or Dotty–make your choice."

Jude was younger than I expected him to be, maybe only in his thirties. But he was stocky, with a thick neck and strong arms showing under his short sleeves. He had close-set eyes and smiled with every one of his teeth.

"Let's go with Dorothy," he said. "I've heard a lot about you." What exactly was *a lot?*

Uncle Ray let Jude take over, but stood nearby as we went through everything–from taking orders to processing payments, carrying food and managing dishes.

He referred to *dubs* five times before I deciphered that he meant waiters and waitresses. W. W. I wondered if there would ever come a time I might say *dubs* in passing and not feel like an idiot.

Aside from the *dubs*, one service assistant was in charge of coffees and desserts each night–and that would be me, to start. I was a little relieved at the thought of remaining tucked behind the coffee machine in the kitchen. That was until I remembered I've only ever made instant coffee and milo milk.

"You'll pick it up fast," Uncle Ray chimed in.

Gradually, my unease lessened and I somehow absorbed some of the unfounded confidence Jude and Uncle Ray seemed to have in me.

When the tour came to its end, Jude told me I wouldn't have to work the night. Thursdays were relatively quiet, apparently, and he already had a service assistant–or *SA*–rostered on. Naturally I felt like a certified idiot having worn my apron … but no one commented on it.

My first shift would be Saturday dinner. I said goodbye to Uncle Ray and thanked Jude. On my way out I heard a low whistle behind me, and paused to glance back.

"Saturday," Darcy said, clucking his tongue. He was polishing cutlery again, and a childish part of me wondered if he'd done so to be closer to the door. "Killer first shift. He's throwing you in the deep end."

I felt my mouth twist nervously, my teeth clamp down on my lip. "I'm a good swimmer," I said, or rather, lied. It was a good line though. I let myself be impressed by it as Darcy grinned and I turned back to the door–

And walked straight into the glass.

My nose took the brunt of it. I hurried outside without daring a backward glance, even when I got to my car.

There were certain moments in my life where the phrase–*only I*, came to mind. Only I would fall asleep on the bus and miss my stop. Only I would tear my dress on the dance floor at my second cousin's wedding last year. Only I would have a boyfriend who'd prefer to party in America than be with me. Only I would walk into a glass door.

I knew it all sounded painfully woeful, but it was how I felt at the time. Like everyone else had learned how to navigate through life without tripping, but I sat that lecture out and was now battling through a test I didn't know the answers to.

My head was a churning mess of *should have*-s and *shouldn't have*-s. I really *should've* seen the glass. Even if I hadn't, I *should've* just made a joke of it, like any normal person would've. I *shouldn't have* run off like that, because that Darcy guy would now see me as a bumbling weirdo and we might even have to work together.

Eventually, moments like this would shrink away into nothing, lose their relevance, but I didn't know that as I drove home that day—trying desperately to convince myself that he hadn't seen me.

3

"So?" Mum was sitting at the kitchen table sewing a button to her cardigan when I came in the door. I shrugged, and her inquiring gaze followed me up the stairs. "Dotty? How'd it go?"

"It was fine," I called back, seeing myself slam into that glass over and over and over.

I fiddled with the ties of my apron and chucked it on the chair in the corner, which was one of those spongy hands with five fingers as the back.

I took a moment to squeeze my eyes shut and allow sufficient cringe time, before changing into the comfiest pyjama pants I owned and forcing the thoughts away.

Kramer was stretched out on my bed. I slid my hand under his soft belly and pulled him onto my lap. I swore sometimes he made himself heavier when he didn't want to move.

I dragged my laptop over my knees and started perusing movies online, settling for a bizarre French one I couldn't even understand *with* subtitles. It followed this young guy who was experiencing all these bizarre flashbacks, although maybe they were flash-forwards, because he was old in them. You watched him seduce all these girls and lead them to his room, which was gross because they were about twenty years younger. I couldn't understand what the point of it all was, but the bizarre sex montage was the final straw.

French films were always a risk. There were some real gems, but you had to dig for them, and you couldn't always unsee the dodgy ones.

I exited out and switched to Facebook. The first photo in my feed loaded slowly, as if my computer was being dramatic, or was kind enough to give me time to scroll past it.

But I didn't. And all of a sudden–there was Cameron with his arm around a girl in the short-est dress I'd ever seen. She was on her tippy toes, planting a kiss on his cheek. Close to his mouth. He looked pretty happy about it too. My gut started to churn.

I shouldn't have been surprised. Though I hated to admit it, Cameron was a serious cutie. No doubt he was living it up wherever he went and meeting girls left, right and centre. My cousin Peter told me once that Americans love Aussies, and the thought hadn't comforted me one bit when Cameron moved.

I jolted as Kramer licked my hand with his sandy tongue, letting me know I'd stopped patting him and he wasn't okay with it. Needy little bugger. I started up again and he purred while I gazed into the laptop screen.

Cameron was the bubbly, outgoing type–the complete opposite of me. Which is probably why he felt okay about leaving in the first place. He'd made it sound like we'd stay together, regardless of the distance. But in hindsight, I don't think that was ever his plan.

That weird film came back to mind, along with a few of the unnecessary, intimate scenes I wished I hadn't seen–particularly as now I was imagining Cameron as the main character with girls tangled in sheets around him.

I shut my laptop and stared into the dark before I could venture into a stalking spree of his new *friend*.

Kramer left my lap to settle by my feet.

Something heavy was weighing on me. Loneliness is too specific a word for the feeling. There shouldn't be a descriptor for it, really. Because it feels like … nothing. Just a hard sort of emptiness. A space where you could exist or not exist and nothing would change.

My mind was fickle. It was either filled with rampant thoughts, or dead silence.

For a moment, I felt as though I was melting into the blackness of my room. Joining the night. And I wondered to myself how long it would take somebody other than Kramer to notice if I never came out of it.

4

The Corner was chaos. Dinner was in full swing when I arrived at seven, with most tables full up. Jude showed me how to log into the system with my fingerprint, and then introduced me to another service assistant who was there to train me at the coffee machine.

Her name was Florence, and I instantly liked her. She had snowy skin and dark hair so long and thick that it swished by her hips like a horse's tail. When she spoke, she looked at me. Really looked, as if she sincerely cared what I might think or say. It was nice, but also stressed me out. Speaking to a stranger who showed no interest was terrifying enough, but speaking to someone attentive sent my usual screening process for conversations into overdrive.

"How long have you worked here?" I asked over the hiss of the milk frothing.

Florence tapped the base of the tin with two fingers. "About a year," she said. "But it feels like forever."

"Corner!" The voice came before the source appeared. *Corner* was what we were apparently

required to say before rounding the *corner* of the kitchen to drop dishes—a warning to avoid collisions. I found the prospect mortifying, but luckily, being tucked away with the coffee machine, I hadn't needed to yell it myself.

A tall guy appeared holding a column of empty glasses. I'd seen him in the main restaurant before I clocked on. His dark hair sprung loosely from a thick bun and he had a hard face with prominent cheekbones.

He set the glasses into the dishwasher and glanced across at me. "Hey, I'm Jesse," he said, so fleetingly that I hadn't got my name out before he was gone again. I couldn't blame him. The restaurant was packing out, and he was the only waiter rostered until eight o'clock.

"Don't worry," Florence said to me, her voice low. "He's only a dick when it's busy." I wouldn't have thought much of the comment, if I hadn't started to note a shift in Flo each time Jesse appeared around the—

"*Corner!*"

Her focus would draw suddenly to the machine, even if we were mid-conversation. Sometimes she'd stop speaking altogether. I wondered what was simmering between them, whether it was disinterest or the exact opposite. I couldn't quite figure it out.

Later in the night a different voice announced itself around the corner. To my dismay—Darcy appeared. He was carrying a stack of dirty plates but his apron was clean. He must've just started.

"Oh, hey," he said, smiling as he met my startled gaze. "It's getting busy out there. Told you Saturday was a nightmare–hi Flo."

"Hey," Florence answered, reaching for a spoon and saucer. "Don't you have soccer?"

"Season's over." He bent to set the dishwasher running. "Just. But Jude's already on my case about working weekends."

"Damn," Florence muttered. "Now you have to suffer with us."

"Yeah." Darcy hesitated a moment. I glanced his way, just as he tapped the wall and left the kitchen.

Maybe I'd been lucky. Maybe he hadn't seen the glass door collision and I was beating myself up for no reason. It wouldn't be the first time.

The night went by swiftly. I learnt that Florence was studying Visual Arts and loved to paint. Mostly portraits. She worked at Corner part-time. She was an only child, like me. I also learnt that she preferred to be called Flo, as I preferred Dot to Dorothy. We came to realise that both names were fairly old-fashioned, but unlike me, she seemed to wear that as a badge of honour.

Jesse and Darcy came and went in rotation–scraping plates behind us and filling the dishwasher between collecting meals. Jude stood at the kitchen window, talking to the head chef and dinging a bell when food was up for the dubs to deliver.

They all appeared to get along well, although whenever Darcy tried to involve me and Flo in conversation, Jesse withdrew.

I found myself in the centre of a storm when I made the mistake of taking a trip to the bathroom. Should've held on. Because before I could make it back to the kitchen, Jude had stopped me and thrust two plates into my hands.

"Table 8," he said urgently, pointing a finger I didn't have time to follow. Then he was back at the kitchen window, swapping a side of fries for veggies. Jesse whooshed by me with a handful of dirty dishes. The plates were weighing down like led the longer I held onto them. Table 8 might as well have been Pluto for all I knew.

I started walking blindly into the tussle, looking left to right. None of the tables were numbered. Just as I wheeled back around to return the dishes to Jude, I felt a tap at my shoulder.

Darcy was there, the faintest trace of a smile working its way into the corners of his eyes. "Where you headed?"

"Table 8." It sounded more like a plea than an answer.

He pointed to the window where an old couple was looking across at me, clearly having spotted their meals in limbo. I felt Darcy's hand light on my back. Propelled by the touch, I glided toward them.

The couple thanked me and I caught them exchanging a bemused look as I set the plates down. Suitably mortified, I made my way back to the kitchen. Darcy stopped me again on the way.

"There's a map on the computer." He gestured back at the stand. "If you're ever unsure about table numbers or whatever."

I liked how he added the, *or whatever*, to make it seem as though it were only a minor detail amongst others I'd understandably missed.

From that point on, the night got better. Making coffees wasn't so bad, apart from the wonky tulips on my lattes, and preparing desserts mostly involved heating cakes in the microwave and drizzling sweet sauces over them. Darcy still hadn't brought up the door incident, so my panic on the subject was gradually easing.

I liked the hustle—snatching docket after docket and prioritizing dessert orders. Flo was still an essential player, but I could feel myself getting better, faster. And having something to keep myself preoccupied made small talk with her easy. I came to think that making friends over a coffee machine might be a real thing.

At nine-thirty Darcy let us know the last customers were leaving. "Jude wants to see you before you go," he added, nodding at me. A nervous twinge skittered down my spine.

I found Jude reclining in a swivel chair in front of a computer, his legs crossed as he clicked away on the mouse. "Oh, Dorothy." He straightened up. "How'd you go tonight?"

"Good." I was half-surprised to realise it was the truth.

"No dramas?"

"No." Surprisingly.

Jude flashed his full smile. "Glad to hear it. It's a rare night when there aren't any."

I inclined my head and went to ask what he meant, then shut my mouth.

"How did Florence go teaching you the ropes?" he asked.

"She was great." I wrung my fingers nervously behind me, wondering where the conversation might be heading.

"Perfect." Jude went back to clicking his mouse over a spreadsheet of some sort. "I'll let Ray know."

Let him know Flo was great? Let him know I didn't have the mental breakdown he predicted?

I waited by the doorway, but Jude didn't look up again. "Can I …"

"Oh, yes." He glanced at me, only briefly. "You can sign off with your fingerprint darling, same as signing in."

Feeling taken aback and mildly flattered by the term of endearment, I went to collect my bag and ran into Jesse at the scanner.

"This was your first shift, right?" he asked, without really looking at me.

"Yeah."

Up close I could see a wild smattering of pale freckles covering his entire face. Rings and studs glinted silver at the top of his ear under a head of hair so thick I wondered how he managed to tame it into that up-do. "So long as you don't swipe our vodka, you'll be right," he said, pressing his forefinger into the scanner.

Assuming he was talking about the girl who was fired before me, I wasn't sure whether to laugh or not, so I changed the subject instead. "How long have you been here?"

"Too long," he said, and finally turned to me with a small smile. It sloped a little to one side. I realised then that there was something appealing about Jesse—a softness in his angular face and a slightly nerdy lilt to his voice.

"I've been working here full-time for about … three years now."

"We can't get rid of him!" Jude called from the office.

Jesse's brows arched high. "Pretty much."

At that moment Flo swept into the back room, and it was as though the air crystallized around us.

She squatted at the lockers along the wall to grab her bag.

"So, you're an expert then," I said, feeling as though I was skating on the ice between them. "Being here for so long."

"Uh, yeah," Jesse murmured. "I mean no, not really. I've got to get going, so—" he raised his hand and sidled past me. Darcy blocked his path at the door.

"Anyone keen for a feed?" he asked, untying his apron and balling it. I couldn't imagine what he meant, considering it was eleven o'clock and everything would be shut. Wouldn't it? Did ordinary people go for *feeds* at this time of night?

"Uh …" Jesse glanced back at me, his eyes skimming over Flo—who was throwing on a knitted cardigan over her work shirt—before returning to Darcy. "What are you thinking?"

Darcy's lips puckered, considering. "Kebabs?"

"Tempting." Jesse turned to me, awaiting an answer. It wasn't often I received an invitation to any social event, even one as spontaneous as this. And it was even less often that whether an outing happened or not rode on my response.

"Would it even be open?" I asked. Both Jesse and Darcy had a laugh at that, and I cringed.

"Always," Darcy said, grinning. "Like, I'm pretty sure if there were a zombie apocalypse, Tommy's Kebabs would still be running hot."

"Oh." I forced a laugh to override my embarrassment. "Okay then, I'll come for a bit."

"I've got to head home," Flo said behind me, turning my chest into a knot. "But you guys go ahead." *Kebabs* with two people I barely knew. *Boys* I barely knew. "See you again, I'm sure." Flo tapped my shoulder and moved past us.

"Why do I never get an invitation?" Jude called from the office.

"Kebabs don't feature in your strict meal plans, do they?" Darcy yelled back. Jude only snorted.

I hurriedly scanned my fingerprint and gathered my things from an open locker before following the boys out.

They'd tilted every chair against the tables, and most of the lights were switched off.

The place felt eerie. And I did too. Meeting new people was a stressful exercise, and meeting new boys without a female buffer was another thing altogether. Best-case scenario would be an awkward dinner. Worst case scenario–murder. At that point, I probably would've preferred the latter.

5

When Cameron left, I tended to play it safe with guys at uni, in that I didn't talk to them much and certainly never sustained friendships with any. If I started to connect with someone, I'd feel guilty, because I knew how much I'd hate it if Cameron were having lunch with cute girls oceans away from me. Turns out, that's probably exactly what he was doing.

But things were different now because there I was, flanked by two exceptionally cute guys on Scarlett Street, heading out for dinner close to midnight.

Tommy's Kebabs was only a short walk from Corner—Darcy had frequented it enough that the owner came to our small, metal table to chat with him. The man—Tommy himself—was loud and crude, and dropped some creepy innuendo about the three of us when he approached. But Darcy shut it down easily, and was able to spin conversation into motion at every pause. Jesse too, although much quieter, was relaxed and quick-witted.

Maybe it had been a bad idea to join them. I wasn't exactly contributing much to the conversation, and

28

to make things worse, I realised too quickly that it was near-impossible to maintain any degree of dignity whilst eating a kebab.

"Just go for it," Darcy commented through a mouthful, as I tapped a napkin to the corner of my lips. "Mess is inevitable."

I sighed and dug in, setting aside my awkwardness as best I could.

"That guy was in again today," Jesse said. His freckles were more obvious in the harsh light of the shop, a smattering of pale and dark spots. "Crazy eyes. Did you see Darc? Sitting by the window."

"Huh." Darcy swallowed a huge mouthful of kebab. "I didn't realise it was him."

"Who?" I asked, hoping I wasn't being overly intrusive.

"We have a few *quirky* regulars," Jesse explained, casting Darcy a wry smile.

"This dude is more than quirky," Darcy added. "Always comes in alone and gets the same meal every time."

I wanted to say—*what's wrong with that?* But I figured they probably couldn't relate. I was sure they had no trouble finding people to go to dinner with.

"His eyes are always bloodshot," Jesse went on. "Probably high on something."

"*Actually* though," chimed Darcy.

I focused on my kebab again, trying to think of something clever to say. I'd decided on a joke about the Corner chef lacing the guy's dinner, when Jesse said–

"We talk about work way too bloody much outside of work." He wiped his hands on his jeans. I noticed that Darcy went for a napkin instead, dragging it over every finger. "Tell us about yourself, Dot," Jesse said. "It's Dot, right?"

I nodded. "Not much to say, really. I'm studying Business at Swinburne, in my second year. I ... I'm an only child?"

"Lucky you," Jesse muttered. I frowned, and he laughed. "I have a little sister, or should I say–a little beast. Just turned ten."

"Wow, you just turned ten?" Darcy feigned shock.

Jesse rolled his eyes. "You'll learn to laugh at Darc's jokes," he said to me. "He tries."

"I do." Darcy smiled brightly. It was a striking look on him–framed in his tanned skin, sandy hair and chocolate-brown eyes. "I have a sister too, but she's older by a few years so we don't cross over much."

There was a prolonged lull in the conversation, during which Jesse flicked on his phone and started scrolling through his Instagram feed.

I decided to broach a potentially dangerous topic, but one I was curious enough about to try on them. "Flo seems nice," I said, stamping a stray piece of lettuce and returning it to my napkin. "Do you all hang out a lot?"

Darcy looked to Jesse, who made an uncertain noise in the back of his throat. "When we can, yeah. She's just …" He cut Darcy a look over his phone. "She isn't my biggest fan."

"Oh." I pretended to appear surprised by the fact.

"Why? Did she say something to you?" Jesse looked at me, suddenly intent.

"No, no." I shook my head for emphasis. "Sorry, I didn't mean to–"

"Don't worry about it," Darcy said. "I don't even understand those two, and I've known them for years."

Jesse reached for Darcy's napkin and threw it at him, half-laughing. "Piss off."

I didn't push for more. Something told me I'd find out soon enough.

———•———

"So tell me, how is Corner treating you?" Uncle Ray asked as he passed me the corn dish.

Truth was, it was treating me well, all things considered. "It's fun," I admitted. "I'm enjoying it."

Mum glowered at me from the other side of the table, as if to say–*I told you so*. I pretended not to have seen.

"We'll get you out serving soon," Uncle Ray said. "You're far too good for coffees, girl."

I tried not to let my terror show. I was perfectly content making coffees, thank you. And I was getting better at it, too. I'd had one more shift under Flo's supervision the other night. Jesse and Darcy weren't working, but I'd met two more dubs. Emma and Reese.

Emma was a vibrant, strawberry-blonde. What she lacked in height, she made up for in candour and loud laughter.

I couldn't work out if Reese was obnoxious or overly friendly. Or both. He wore round glasses and carried himself with an unfair amount of ease. Apparently he was in his final year studying architecture. I'd always thought of architects as quiet souls who spent most of their time indoors sketching floor plans to folk music. Reese defied the stereotype. At Corner he alternated bartender duties with Jude, and it was evident that they both knew how to entertain.

Reese and Emma seemed close. Whenever they'd crossed paths in the kitchen, they were either in fits of laughter or on the verge of it. It didn't take much for one to tip the other over the edge. Flo told me she always wondered why they hadn't dated. By the end of the shift, I'd found myself wondering the same thing.

"Why don't *you* work for Uncle Ray?" I fired at Peter. He was at the table's head, beside me.

"Because I have a real job," he said. "No offence." It was a standard Peter comment. He worked at a bank and seemed to think that handling money all day meant he had a lot, which set him on some higher pedestal to the rest of us.

Don't get me wrong—he turned out well, considering his crazy mother jumped ship when he was a kid. We didn't talk about Aunty Rhea much, none of us did, but I knew he was pretty bitter about it. So, I forgave him for the fact that he hadn't inherited Uncle Ray's genuine humility, and for the smoking. There were other things that could've gone wrong that hadn't.

"Hey, you might take on the business one day kiddo," said Uncle Ray, jabbing his fork across me at Peter. "Better start showing an interest in it."

Peter made a face. "No thanks."

I smiled as Uncle Ray sighed heavily. It was a conversation they'd had plenty of times before. But even I knew Peter was too lazy to manage a chain.

"You want to crack backs with me one day, sweetie?" Dad said to me. Before you think my Dad is a psycho, context—he was a chiropractor.

"No thanks," I echoed Peter, and he gave me a wink. At this stage, I wasn't sure what I was going to do with my Business degree, but I was fairly certain it wouldn't involve back cracking.

"Well the kids seem to like you," Uncle Ray said, giving me a wink more obvious than Peter's. "At least that's what they tell me."

My jaw fell slack. "You asked if they *liked* me?"

"Of course! I'd ask them for their opinions no matter who I'd hired."

Except I wasn't anyone. *I'm your niece*, I almost snapped. Maybe they'd even assume I'd instructed him to find out what they thought of me. How mortifying.

Peter went outside for a cigarette while Mum brought out the dessert—an apple crumble she'd bought frozen and heated up. As I watched the ice cream melt over the pastry, I wondered how much Uncle Ray knew about the dubs at Corner. Darcy and Jesse and Flo. Even Emma and Reese. If I was anyone else, I'd just ask.

What was the beef between Flo and Jesse? What did he think of Darcy? Had any of them dated before?

But the questions remained lodged in my throat, and although I knew Uncle Ray wouldn't have minded, I convinced myself it was none of my business.

———◆———

That night I pulled out the skeleton in my closet. That's what Dad called it. Except, it wasn't in my closet. They were in plain sight on my desk in black display folders. I'd accumulated *hundreds* of business cards over the years. Literally.

Above them was a shelf of knick-knacks–clusters of little mementos from vaguely significant days and places. The shelf had blended with my room's landscape and I mostly overlooked it, but I flicked through the business cards on occasion. There was something therapeutic about it. The neat blocks of colour and text from places I'd been or wanted to go.

I passed an old Corner card Uncle Ray gave me a few years back. I was fairly sure they'd updated the design since. I'd have to swipe a new one during my next shift.

My thoughts slipped to Darcy. His big, warm smile and brown eyes, which were dark and bright at the same time. I thought of how he'd included me in the kebabs plan, and how he said that mess was inevitable, like if I had aioli and lettuce all over my face it wouldn't make a difference. And it was then, sweeping my thumb over the dated Corner card and pondering those kebabs–that I realised how much I liked him already.

6

Extra pawpaw ointment was required today–I knew my lips would crack within the hour. They always dried out when I was anxious. So they were dry most of the time.

But today was extra terrifying, because I would be learning how to wait on tables. I even bought a cheap black shirt from Target before my shift started. I'd noticed most of the others wore black.

Uncle Ray was there, likely for my benefit. But his presence only made my nerves jump around even more, because what if I screwed up? I felt the pressure closing in on me the moment I saw him.

"You'll kill it, girl," he said, slapping my shoulder so hard I almost toppled over. "They'll love you. How could they not love you?"

Darcy was working, but Jude said I'd be shadowing Jesse most of the night. I didn't mind that either. I'd rather Darcy remain ignorant of my general, social incompetence.

"Just listen to how I greet them," Jesse said, leaning against the metal kitchen window. "It's easy." And at that, he pushed off the counter and approached the table nearest us. Four men sat around it, menus raised. I would have felt less nervous approaching a table of orcs on dinner break in Mordor. That was the thing about customers, and people in general. They were opaque. At least orcs were upfront with their intentions.

Jesse breezed over to the men like it was—as he said—easy, and I trailed behind him with my heart pounding. I listened to the way he phrased the questions and watched how far he stood from the table, the way he moved.

When we came away, he cast me a smirk. "See? Easy."

"For you, maybe," I said, chewing my lip. It was a bold admission of my feelings of inadequacy, and Jesse seemed to realise it judging by his bemused, hitched brow.

We went through most of the night like this—Jesse leading and me in tow. Thankfully Uncle Ray mostly stayed in the back office with Jude.

My least favourite part was having to yell, "*Corner!*" whenever we walked into the kitchen. I couldn't bring myself to match the volume of the other dubs. I knew there was a practical reason for it, but I never liked raising my voice in public, even if it was just to get somebody's attention.

It was about nine-fifteen when Jesse suggested I tend to a table of teenaged girls alone. They looked younger than me, but that didn't help much. I knew how unforgiving girls could be even at my age.

I didn't want Jesse to watch me approach them, so when he moved off to deliver meals to table 4, I seized the opportunity.

After hovering over the girls for a few seconds, I cut in with, "Hi, have you had a look at the menus yet?" It was clunky, but not terrible.

As I scribbled down their orders, my attention snagged on Darcy. He was filling water glasses at the drinks stand nearby, smiling at me. My flow—if there was such a thing—faltered, and I had to ask the last girl to repeat her order.

I took their menus and shuffled to the computer beside Darcy without looking at him, feeling both triumphant and embarrassed.

"You're a natural," he mused behind me.

I held up my notepad and started tapping the order into the touch screen. "And you're a good liar," I said, my cheeks flaring up.

Darcy laughed. "I'm actually a terrible liar, believe it or not."

"That's something a good liar would say." It was unusual for me to slip so easily into banter with someone I knew so little. Despite the rapidly tightening knot in my stomach, Darcy made it relatively easy.

"What are you searching for?" he asked, moving to my side as I flicked through the sub menus on the screen.

"How do you select no cheese?"

"They don't want cheese? Who are these people?" Darcy craned his neck to glare at the table of girls. "Send them away," he said with a flick of his hand. I laughed a little too loudly and tried to stifle the sound, resulting in a highly attractive snort. Darcy only smiled before breezing on to show me how to add changes to a meal.

That was when Jesse returned to check up on me. He seemed impressed by my progress and palmed off two more of his tables.

I'd just set down heavy pasta dishes for a middle-aged couple when I spotted a familiar face at the door. At first glance I was almost relieved to see it, but that didn't last long. Because there was *my Dad*, crossing his arms as he surveyed the room.

Our eyes met. He must've detected my horror, because he rocked back on his heels and laughed at the pitched ceiling. And then Darcy was there, holding one finger up as if to ask *table for one?* I rushed across to them.

"What are you doing here?"

"Hello to you too, daughter I'm so happy to see," Dad said. He gave Darcy a look, like he was in on the joke.

"Dad," I groaned. "This isn't the best time." First shift working tables and here he was, readying himself to scrutinize me.

"What do you mean?" Again he looked to Darcy, who was standing back a little trying to keep a straight face. "I'm just here for a meal. So please, lead the way sir."

"The man needs his dinner," Darcy said, shrugging at me before taking Dad to one of the few remaining tables.

Don't get me wrong—I adored my Dad. But he thoroughly enjoyed getting involved in my life, sometimes a little too much. Back at school he would take days off work to attend my sports carnivals. I never even won anything, but he came every year.

It was an obnoxious complaint, that my Dad should love me so much he'd want to be a part of everything I did, but I couldn't shrug away the irritation. Especially not tonight, when I was already on edge about keeping on track.

I tried to draw a black bar over him in my mind to pull focus to my tables. But not only was Dad hard to ignore—Darcy was too. And *Darcy* was minding *Dad's* table. I caught them looking across at me a few times, both grinning. Nodding. Gesturing around the restaurant. What were they talking about?

I was at the stand filling glasses with water from the tap when I felt a tap on my shoulder. I turned and saw no one. So I spun the other way and there was Darcy, smirking.

"Very funny," I said.

"I know. Hey, your Dad's really cool."

"Oh boy."

"Nah seriously." Darcy came up beside me and took two empty glasses from the top shelf of the stand. "He told me I look like a young Liam Neeson."

Of course he did.

"I don't think I've ever seen a young Liam Neeson," I said, an attempt to bypass Dad's overfamiliar observation.

Darcy gestured to his face. "Apparently you have."

I stepped away from the tap and tried to get my fingers around the three glasses I'd filled.

"Let me show you something," Darcy said, and proceeded to demonstrate how to carry them all in one hand. He told me to hold out mine, and then he attempted to set the glasses into it, our fingers brushing every now and then. We soon figured out that my palm was much smaller than his—too small for the job. So he let me go back to the awkward, two-handed approach.

I moved off to deliver the drinks and my gaze caught Dad's along the way. He averted his eyes quickly, but I figured he'd probably been watching me and Darcy. Making assumptions I'd be sure to hear about later. Yet another reason I wished he hadn't come in.

Jesse passed me on my way back, walking fast and purposefully. "You doing all right?"

"Yep," I lied, my forehead prickling with sweat. There were a hundred things to do for my allocated tables and yet all I could think about was Dad in the corner and Darcy's fingers grazing mine around those glasses.

———◆———

"Missed you in the kitchen today," Flo told me as we grabbed our bags at the end of the shift.

"I'd much rather be there," I said. "People are scary." It slipped out before I could stop it, so I laughed—hoping she'd think it was a joke.

But she gave me this knowing look. "I know right? That's why I've never asked to be trained as a dub. Too much pressure."

I considered telling her my Dad had come in and that had only exacerbated the trauma of the night, but decided to let it slide.

We walked together into the main restaurant, past Darcy and Jesse who were closing up—Darcy tilting chairs against tables and Jesse tying rubbish bags.

"Great job today," Jesse said to me, but my "thanks" fell against his back as he swung the rubbish over a shoulder and crossed the room. I presumed the rapid departure had something to do with Flo's presence, though I still didn't know what exactly.

Darcy was taking off his apron as we passed him. "Next time we'll leave all the tables to you," he said. "Also, tell your Dad I say hi."

I gave a strangled sort of laugh in response. Flo and I made for the door and she paused before opening it, turning to whisper, "Looks like you have a cheer squad."

———◆———

Last-minute decisions were a rarity for me. Not because I couldn't think fast enough, but because I thought too fast, too much.

I leaned against the steering wheel, watching as Flo pulled a beanie over her ears and crossed the road.

"I catch the bus most nights," she had said moments ago, before we parted at the Corner entrance. I knew there was no obligation to drop her home, but that slightly uneasy feeling in my chest had been growing since she said it.

And so I drove out from the car park and pulled up alongside her, drawing down the window. "Hey, I can drop you home."

She smiled. "Oh no, I don't want to put you out."

"Not at all," I said, beckoning with a forced, blasé wave. "It's no biggy."

I saw her hesitation, and wondered if I'd messed up–if *she* was the one who felt obligated now. Maybe she would much rather take the bus and not have to worry about making conversation. I could relate to that.

But before I could reassure her I didn't mind either way, she was clambering in, setting her bag by her feet.

"Thanks, I really appreciate it. I'll direct you–it isn't far from here. Thank you so much."

"No worries." My heart was racing, but that wasn't unusual. It always did that when I entered into conversation with someone I didn't know well. Sometimes I wondered if other people had the same reaction. But asking would mean admitting to it myself, and I'd probably sound like a weirdo.

"How was Jesse tonight?" Flo posed the question casually, but it was overly saturated with sweetness, like she'd been cooking it up for a while. "I mean, did everything go all right? Take a left here."

"Yeah." I flicked on the indicator. "It was fine. He was good." I knew that was hardly an adequate response. Only, dwelling on what Flo hoped to hear about Jesse had me panicking. I tried a little harder, going for the honest approach. "It seems so easy for him. Like, there's zero awkwardness when he approaches tables."

"He can be pretty awkward," Flo interposed. She was smiling a little. "We've had a tonne of drama recently–you've probably noticed how he acts around me."

I commanded my brow into a frown but kept my eyes on the road. "What do you mean?"

Flo sighed and pointed ahead. "It's just the next right," she said, before clearing her throat. "So there was this awards night, recently. A big event where all the Corner workers met in one store for drinks. Your uncle puts it on once a year."

I did recall Uncle Ray mentioning something along those lines, a while back. It was strange now hearing it from someone on the inside.

"So it ended up being me, Jesse, Darc, Reese and Em." She paused, as if giving me time to digest the names. "We went out afterwards, to this bar in the city, and Jesse and I hooked up."

"Oh." I wasn't surprised.

"I mean, I'd always thought he was really cool, and we'd known each other for years. But we weren't super close–not until that night. We went back to his place and talked for hours. So … there I was thinking it might be the start of something, but turns out we were still only friends, in his mind. Turn right at Marilla Street."

"That's—" I swallowed, carefully thinking through the right words to say. "That's tough."

"Mhm." Flo pulled her beanie down further over her ears and ran her fingers through her hair, which slipped through them like silk.

"Do you still want to be his friend?" I asked.

She took her time to consider the question, enough to leave me sweating over whether I might have overstepped. "I don't know," she said at last. "I really don't know. He was kind of a dick to me. But I still think he's great. We have tons of common interests. He's really into his photography, and I love to paint. I know they're different things, but ..."

"You're both artists," I said.

Another long sigh. "Kind of, yeah. I just don't know what his hesitation was. It's not like he was dating anyone else—it's the house with the big tree out front," Flo said, gesturing ahead. I pulled over in front of a small, brick unit. "What do *you* think of him?"

"Oh." I pulled the handbrake and shook my head. "I'm not interested in Jesse."

Flo laughed, a pretty sound that came swiftly, as if stealing her breath without her permission. "I didn't mean that."

I tried to laugh with her. "Oh, sorry."

"It's all right. What do you think of him though? You went to dinner with the boys, right?"

"Yeah." I chewed my lip, wondering how much to say. Her eyes were wide and earnest. I had a fairly reliable gauge on people, and she seemed trustworthy so far. "Jesse mentioned that you aren't his biggest fan, but that's all he said."

"Aren't his biggest fan?" Flo huffed. "Bullshit. He'll tell himself anything to avoid the truth."

I decided to stop there, not that I had much more to offer. It seemed a sore topic.

"And Darc–I can tell he likes you." Flo puckered her lips as if to conceal a smile. "Not many newbies get the kebab invite so soon."

"Well, I like him too," I said, forcing my tone into a lightness I didn't feel.

"Ah, Darcy." Flo sighed. "He's been with Nina way too long. I get the impression she enjoys bossing him around, and he takes it 'cos he's such a nice guy." Her eyes fell back on me, glinting in the streetlight. "He deserves someone better, in my opinion."

My heart had sunk like a stone, leaving my chest hollow. I tried to tell myself it didn't matter. So, Darcy had a girlfriend. It wasn't like we'd established anything beyond polite small talk.

So what if he was a cutie? There were other cuties … somewhere. Besides, it was completely irrational to think anything would happen between me and the first guy who bothered to overlook my awkwardness.

"Alrighty." Flo grabbed her bag. "I should go—but thank you so much for dropping me off."

"Anytime," I said, tapping the wheel. "Oh, and don't worry about that Jesse stuff. I won't say anything."

Flo hesitated, pursing her lips for a beat. "If it comes up with him, I don't mind if you mention that I'm still, you know, interested." That took me by surprise. I felt suddenly like a mediator—and I knew I was hardly the best person for the job. I was a solid confidant, but negotiating emotionally turbulent scenarios wasn't my specialty. "It's just frustrating not knowing why," Flo said, her hand against the open car door. "But, I'm sure he'll avoid the topic at all costs." She laughed then, but I doubted she found it even a little bit funny.

"I'll let you know if he does," I told her, unsure if I was prematurely breaking Jesse's confidence by making the promise.

I waited for Flo to reach her front door before I left. It struck me then how strange it was that someone so pretty and easygoing would continue pining over a guy who had dealt her such a blatant rejection. If Jesse had been interested in her, he would've made it clear then, or since, wouldn't he? And now I'd got myself into a position where I might have to reinforce that rejection.

How did that happen?

See, this is why it was easier to be antisocial.

And Darcy–taken. Not a surprising revelation, really. But still, I felt a little deflated by it.

Thinking back on those problems would become therapeutic, in a way. They would feel light. Approachable. Like secure boards under my feet when everything else threatened to slip away.

7

"I told him not to go." Mum's hands were raised in a splay of innocence. She and Dad had been watching an episode of MasterChef when I stormed in and descended upon them.

Dad shook his head. "What does it matter, Dotty?"

"It's not—it's just, I was *already* stressed out."

"You were great!"

I tossed my bag against the wall. "Dad …"

"I was curious to see you in action."

"Well, I wish you'd given me warning."

He waved away my concern, and then said, "That Darcy fella seems nice."

"Oh boy." I flopped back into the single couch. "*This* is why."

"Why what?" Dad frowned at me—then at Mum, as if she might interpret for him. He could be so clueless.

"Okay," she said, patting his knee. "Next time we'll let Dotty know beforehand, won't we?" All of a sudden I felt like a child she was trying to coax out of a near tantrum, and that made me ease up a little because I didn't want to be that child.

"You should've seen this Darcy kid, Kat," Dad said. "A young Liam Neeson! Spitting image."

At that, I picked up my bag and went upstairs.

———◆———

The last time I saw Cameron was at the airport. I'd driven him there and we had lunch at Macca's before it was time for him to leave. I felt so sick I could barely stomach a bite of my cheeseburger, but I told him I just wasn't hungry and he ate the rest of it.

At the gate, he'd gathered me up in his arms and squeezed me close. Cameron was tall and lanky and his hugs were like having a warm blanket draped around your shoulders. He smelt like the cologne I'd bought him for his birthday, and when he kissed me it was fierce and long like it pained him to let go.

So much time had passed, but it was disconcerting thinking back to that moment. It was meant to be a goodbye with a promise. *We'll see each other soon*. But within weeks, Cameron decided it would be the last time he ever held me like that.

A relationship and a friendship spanning years, grinding to a halt right there in the airport that day. If I'd known what was to come, I wouldn't have held on so tight.

8

For a walk-in fridge, there wasn't much space to walk in. I gritted my teeth against the cold, scouring the shelves for tubs. A *white tub*, Reese had said, when he'd ask me to hunt for more ice cream in the kitchen. He was running low at the bar and choc-malteser milkshakes were a Corner specialty. This was an emergency.

I heard the door clang behind me, but kept searching until I finally spotted a few white tubs on the highest shelf. I had to jump a little to reach them.

The container was so cold it burnt my arm, but I tucked it close anyway and pushed against the door. It didn't budge.

Was there a handle? I ran my hands over something that looked like it might be, and jiggled it. Nothing.

Dread gripped my gut and twisted. I pushed hard against the steel. Then again, harder. The walls started caving in and my breath caught. I thumped my shoulder against the door with such force my bones rattled.

"Hey!" I forced a casual tone to mask the panic. "Is anyone—can someone open this door?"

My teeth chattered and goosebumps prickled along my arms. I was about to yell again when the door sprung open and I tumbled out, dropping the tub. The bald chef—whose name escaped me—helped me to my feet. He was cursing, and I thought it might've been directed at me and my stupidity until he said, "I'm so sorry love, I didn't see you go in. Thought I left it open!"

"Oh." I bent to collect the tub of ice cream, trembling. "It's okay." I didn't want to consider what might've happened if he hadn't heard me. How long did it take to freeze to death?

I passed Darcy at the stand and felt his eyes follow me. "You all G?"

"Mhm." I tried to smile. "Yep." But humiliation was falling over me like a heavy, sinking cloud.

I already felt small. Even if the reason was fairly understandable, it didn't help when other people couldn't see me either.

9

Swinburne was a frenzy in my final week. People sat in clusters across benches and grass, cramming for final exams and assignments. I was amongst them, sitting on a bench against the wall of the building where my last Business Management exam would be held. I still had an hour to go over my notes.

But they didn't hold my attention for long. My focus drifted up to the people milling around on the grass, speed-walking across the pavement or bustling to and from the café opposite.

I got thinking about the complex web of stories intermingling in crowded places like this. How it was a point of intersection for every person who passed through.

In preferring to avoid social scenarios, I tended to eliminate those points of intersection. I'd talked to more people at Corner than I had all year here at uni, but only because the job had been thrust upon me.

"Hey, mind if I sit here?" I jumped at the voice. A girl with purple hair was standing in front of me, pointing to the free edge of the bench.

"Yeah, sure." I slid across to make more room for her.

She pulled a laptop from her bag and set it over her knees. The case was battered and even the computer was scuffed at the corners.

I summoned an ounce of courage enough to ask, "You here for Business Management?"

"Nah," she said, and I caught a glimpse of a black stud in her tongue. "I study Psych."

"Oh, cool." I went back to my notes, swallowing back my embarrassment.

"Just had a tutorial, but my exam's tomorrow," the girl said. "I have to remember like twenty notable figures in the field and what they each offered, but I have the worst memory."

"Mine isn't great either," I told her, although that wasn't exactly true. If anything, my memory was too good.

"And nobody seems to question Freud," she went on, turning to me with this exasperated look. "He was kind of a massive creep."

She was one of those people whose face was open and easy to read. Like what she said was really what she was thinking. And I was a stranger. I wished it could be effortless for me too.

"I don't know much about him," I said. "Just that he had some weird ideas."

"Look, they're not all crazy. But it's like, what must he have been thinking about to reach those conclusions? You know?"

She went on to talk through some of his theories, a few vulgar enough to have me glancing around in the hope that no one was listening in.

Eventually it was time for my exam, so I said goodbye and left her on the bench. I didn't even know her name. But it didn't matter. Even the smallest intersection could bring your feet a little closer to the ground and leave you feeling like the world wasn't rotating on without you.

10

They took a table near the door—in hindsight, likely with intention—and timed their walkout when I was fiddling with other orders at the stand. It was only Darcy and I working that night, with Flo on coffees in the kitchen. The group had been pleasant enough when I served them, two guys and two girls—all in their twenties if I had to guess.

Darcy nudged my shoulder at the stand. "Hey, they paid, yeah?" He gestured outside. The group was clambering into a car.

No. They certainly did not.

"*Shivers.*" I ran.

Darcy's bewildered laughter faded behind me as I skated across the timber slates and flung the door open.

"Hey!" I called, waving at the car. But it was already spinning away, its wheels screeching on the concrete. I watched it until it disappeared around the corner, then paced a little, chewing on my lip as I considered what to do next. My heart was pounding in my ears from the panic and the mad dash.

"Bastards," Darcy muttered behind me. He was looking out at the road. "It happens occasionally. Don't worry. Unlucky for your first solo shift, but—it does happen."

I tried to rid my face of the disappointment creeping over me. "What now then?"

"We'll tell Jude," he said. "But it'll be okay. Don't stress—you look stressed."

Darcy touched my arm, before quickly withdrawing it into a wave and beckoning me inside. I felt the place where his fingers had been like a brand.

Unfortunately, that particular occurrence wasn't the only less than ideal situation over the next week at Corner. There was the time I attempted to serve an elderly woman her bruschetta, and the toast slid right off the plate and into the open handbag by her feet.

"I thought she might have asked for takeaway," Jesse had said when we were closing up.

It had made me smile, despite the fact that the look on that poor lady's face as her meal sailed on by would haunt me while I slept that night.

There was also the time I served garlic bread to a young mother and her toddler, only to have her approach me at the stand with steam billowing out her ears. She had specified dairy free meals—but I hadn't remembered the butter on the bread. She was shrieking, right in my face.

Emma–the bubbly, strawberry blonde–was working with me that night. She bustled to my side, still holding three milkshakes and probably having registered my state of frozen shock, and calmly told the customer that we'd arrange another serve without butter. It was what I should've done, but I couldn't seem to articulate anything more than a stutter.

"Garlic bread without butter?" Emma whispered once the lady had returned in a huff to her table. "That's just bread. Plain bread. Some people, I swear …"

With my uni semester finally over, I picked up two more shifts for Uncle Ray. I was working four days–rostered with Jesse or Emma during the week, and Darcy on Saturday nights.

Flo stayed in the kitchen during most of the shifts. I only saw her fleetingly afterwards–which is why it came as such a surprise when she suggested we get ice cream after our Wednesday lunch shift. I suspected her true intentions were to get information out of me about Jesse. But she was setting herself up for disappointment, because he hadn't mentioned her at all since the kebabs night.

We followed the main road and cut down a side street. I hadn't known the place existed, probably because the only indicative signage was a faded board on the footpath.

"Don't be deceived," Flo said as we approached, as if reading my thoughts. "They have the best ice cream in Melbourne. Trust me." She coiled her ponytail around her hand. "Like, I'm pretty sure it was actually rated the best on Trip Advisor or something."

She chose choc-mint and I went with cookies and cream. I also swiped a business card, which might as well have been a napkin with a number on it.

We took a seat at the only rickety table outside the shop, digging into our cups.

"I feel like you've been well and truly initiated at Corner," she said, smacking her lips. "If you can survive a table pulling a runner and a customer yelling at you over some kitchen mistake, you can survive anything."

"Don't forget the bruschetta fiasco." Or being locked in the fridge. I shuddered at the memory.

Flo let out this low snort that defied her elegance and made me like her even more. "I wish I'd seen it."

"No, you don't." I swallowed a spoonful of ice cream and found myself wondering if this was the first real friend I'd made since Cameron left. It was hard to make lasting friends at uni. Really it was dependent on who you happened to sit next to for the first few tutorials. And even then, you barely had enough time to learn their name before they decided to skip five lectures and you never saw them again.

Apart from kebabs, the last time I went out with a friend like this was close to three years ago. My high school crew. I'd almost forgotten how it felt to sit across from someone simply to enjoy their company. How it didn't matter what you did. The ice cream, for example, was irrelevant. We were digging into it like it was the only reason we were there, but it wasn't.

I let myself enjoy that sentiment, until …

"Have you spoken much to Jesse?" Flo skated her spoon around the edge of her ice cream, collecting the stray chocolate flakes without looking up at me.

"Uh, here and there," I said, unable to ease the disappointment from my rapidly tightening chest. A friend with an agenda, it seemed. Did that still count?

Flo nodded, still not lifting her gaze.

"He hasn't brought anything up. About you," I clarified.

Those pale blue eyes finally levelled with me. "Oh, I just meant in general." Oh, I bet. "Anyway, you're finished with uni now, right?"

"Mhm." I sighed. "Finally."

"You don't like it?"

"Well–" I put my ice cream on the table and cleared my throat. "It's a Business degree, so I didn't expect it to be a circus, but it's *very* dry. And I guess I'm waiting for it to get interesting, because I can't stay this bored forever."

Flo nodded, knowingly. "It's crazy how work dominates everything. Like, I know we need money to survive, but that need kind of snatches a huge portion of your life. So, I've always thought, if it's going to steal so much of my time, I might as well enjoy it."

I realised then that I was chewing my lip hard, and forced myself to stop. I wanted to ask her how she planned to earn money with her painting, but I wasn't sure how to phrase it in a way that didn't sound condescending. I was genuinely curious.

"I think Business has the potential to be interesting," Flo went on, and I wondered if she had also second-guessed what she'd said to me. "In some ways, it is what you make it."

I hoped she was right.

On an impulse, I blurted, "I'd love to see your paintings."

Flo laughed, a little awkwardly. Maybe it was too much, too soon. Maybe she could see how pleased I was to have gained some semblance of a friend with relative ease, and now I was scaring her away.

"I'm trying to get better at showing people," she said. I noticed that her voice changed a little. Dropped into a tone that felt closer to the real her. "Sometimes it can feel like baring your soul, but I *do* need to get used to that if I want to sell my work." I nodded and waited for a consensus. "So, sure." She smiled. "You can come have a look now, if you'd like."

We headed back to the Corner car park, finishing our ice creams along the way. I remembered most of the route to Flo's house, with only one or two nudges.

She didn't mention Jesse again, and I was glad.

"Okay, so, warning—my room looks like the aftermath of a nuclear explosion," Flo said at the door. "I justify it by saying artists are entitled to mess."

"Makes sense," I said, following her inside. We moved through a cluttered lounge room of squashy couches and beanbags, a low television and coffee table, and a huge canvas over the back wall. It was a sun setting over a beach, all pink and orange and yellow, the lines so defined I'd probably call it abstract.

I was going to ask if she had painted it, but Flo was already disappearing down a narrow hallway. And I didn't need to anyway, because when I entered her room the answer was evident.

It was a long, narrow space with a wide window overlooking a garden of colourful pansies. A small bed was pressed against the farthest wall, as though sleep had been forced to make room for the easels and canvases and palettes scattered across the floor.

Flo took a seat on a wooden stool near the largest canvas, which was covered in waves of colour. A trembling rainbow. "This one isn't finished yet," she said. "I was going for the ocean's surface, and I wanted it to look iridescent, like a bubble that shines blue and pink from certain angles. But I think I need different paints."

I ran my gaze over the other paintings on thinner paper, and the scattered rough sketches. I say rough, but they were impressive too. There were landscapes, vibrant and moody, but also faces. Portraits. I was drawn to them most of all.

My eyes snagged on a sketch that looked suspiciously familiar—wild hair tied back, freckles, a fine nose and studded ears. Flo bent and gathered it up along with a few others, laying it facedown on the small desk behind the easel. It might have looked casual enough if her cheeks hadn't turned flaming red.

I stepped forward for a closer look at a painting of electricity towers silhouetted against a rose-pink sky, shrinking over grassy fields.

"Flo, these are seriously good," I told her. And I meant it.

It was typical for me to feel strangely vulnerable around people, whether it was warranted or not. Questioning every word and look, eternally concerned how I might be perceived. But there in Flo's room, surrounded by her work—her innermost emotions splashed across paper and canvas—I didn't feel like the vulnerable one.

"They're all a bit hodge-podge," she said, a shade of blush in her voice. "But you get the idea. I like to experiment with colour."

I stepped back and felt something hard under my heel. A tube of black paint, I realised, scooting it to the right with my foot. That's when another stray sketch caught my attention.

It was split in two by a thick line, a figure peering across the divide as if to see around it.

"Ah yeah." Flo grabbed it off the floor and smiled. "I want to paint this one eventually."

A part of me wanted to ask what it represented, but I felt that since Flo had opened her soul up to me, I needed to tread carefully around it.

"Flo?" The voice rose from down the hallway.

"In my room!" she answered. "I have a friend over."

I felt a triumphant rush of warmth run through me. *Friend.*

A tall man appeared in the doorway. He wore a brimmed hat with grey, longish hair sprouting out underneath. "Ah, here's a new face," he said, jamming his hands into his pockets. "Corner or uni?"

"Corner," Flo answered, as I gave him one of my best awkward smiles. "This is Dorothy, Dad."

"Hi," I said, a little surprised she'd used my full name.

"John." He ducked his head in a friendly nod. "Thought Flo might have snuck another boy in here."

Flo waved at him. "Okay, thanks Dad, bye!"

"Remember that time?" he said, evidently unperturbed by the dismissal. "You were in year … eleven, weren't you? He must've come in through her window, Dorothy, because we certainly didn't hear the door."

"Again, Dad? He came through the door!" It was the most animated I'd seen Flo—her voice lifting and her eyes alight with defiance.

Flo's Dad raised his hands. "We didn't hear it, that's all. We would've heard it."

"He loves bringing this up in front of people," she said to me in a feigned whisper.

"Window," he said, pointing at her with narrowed eyes before disappearing from view and calling down the hallway. "Don't mess with my marbles, I've got a while yet before I lose them."

"Door!" Flo yelled after him, and then she leant in to me with a small, conspiratorial smile. "It was the window, but he can never know."

The Saturday night frenzy was in full swing–Darcy, Emma and I spinning by each other with the occasional smile or odd conversation at the stand.

Working a shift at Corner meant keeping up with a series of rapidly accumulating layers: take water to table 3 and get them another fork because the baby threw one on the floor, meals to table 2, the old lady wanted another napkin, clear dishes from table 1 before the next booking at nine o'clock. Remember everything, and you were okay. Miss one thing and quite frankly you were screwed.

Thankfully, my only mishap was forgetting to take water to table 3. They must have asked Darcy for it again, because I saw him delivering five glasses to the table without saying a word to me.

Emma hosed down the dishwasher after close and met Darcy, Flo and me in the back office to sign off. It was Emma who proposed we shouldn't let the night end there.

"The park down the road?" she suggested eagerly. "We went once before, remember? With the whole crew. I can tell Reese and Jesse to meet us."

"I'm out," Darcy said, and despite myself, my stomach dropped a level. "But I'll be down next time."

"Argh." Emma huffed. "Nina stealing you away?" *Nina.* I've never liked the name Nina.

Darcy shrugged and swung his bag over a shoulder. "Let me know if you're there late. I might meet you."

I considered his evasion of Emma's Nina comment. Then I considered how silly I was for considering it.

Emma turned on me. "Dot? Flo? Park hang?"

We looked at each other and seemed to agree at the same time. It was a nice moment, like we were both waiting for the other to commit before we did.

Friendship didn't happen all at once, but sometimes it felt that way. It could take a series of moments to really connect with a person, but then it could take only one for you to realise how happy you were to have met them.

Before we left the restaurant, I ducked my head into Jude's office. "Hey, are there any Corner business cards floating around?"

Jude inclined his head. "If you want my number Dorothy, all you have to do is ask." The comment would've made me squirm a little if he hadn't added, "I'll give you a few—in case you meet any nice guys I might like." Ah, well there was a question answered. I wanted to tell him that if I met a nice guy I certainly wouldn't be palming him off, but I just grinned and said, "Deal."

They were a new design, as I suspected. Thick, black cards with *CORNER* embossed in gold across the front. Much classier than the flimsy, old version I had in my collection. *Well done, Uncle Ray.*

Darcy had left by the time I trotted outside. Flo and Emma were waiting for me there and Emma led us to her car, insisting we should car-pool.

She called Reese on the way, and Flo and I listened in silence to their excessively loud conversation, whereby Emma informed him if he didn't meet us at the park she'd be forced to tell Jude about the time a customer found one of Reese's hairs in their pasta. At the time, Emma had pretended she was the manager and apologised to the customer to avoid throwing Reese under the bus–Flo whispered in my ear from the back seat.

Jesse was Emma's next victim. I had to resist peering back at Flo to gauge her reaction when he picked up. She clearly liked the guy, but I wasn't certain she wanted him to be involved in this plan.

"Hey Em, what's happening?" He sounded tired.

"We're meeting at Marley Park right now and you're coming."

"Oh, sweet." Jesse let out a sleepy chuckle. "Why exactly?"

"Because it's fun and spontaneous."

I glanced at Emma, clutching the wheel, an expectant smile lighting up her face. Her hair was tied in a chaotic bun almost to her forehead and it looked redder under the traffic lights.

I didn't know her all too well, and yet here I was, in her car on the way to Marley Park to do God knows what. What did groups of friends do in dark parks?

"Fair enough," came Jesse's reply. "Who's in?"

"Me, Dot, Flo and Reese."

There was a length of silence. "Uh, cool." Again—I fought the urge to look around at Flo. "Yeah, I'll come."

"Meet us at the playground with the hammock swing," Emma fired, beaming now. She certainly knew how to bring people together. If she was aware of anything to do with Jesse and Flo's history, she didn't let on. I tended to skate on the ice between them, but she was cracking it open with a sledgehammer.

———•———

It was one of those summer nights where the air was thick and humid with a cool breeze to break it. They were my favourite, because they held this buzz of possibility. The nights that whispered promises, only to surprise you with something you never could have expected. It was something about the cloak of an inky sky dotted with glittering stars. There was magic in it. Of course, this was hardly a substantiated, scientific fact. But I often found treasures in nights like those.

The park was pitch black aside from a single lamp nearby the playground. The three of us got out of the car and Emma started racing forward. To the swings, I realised, following the line of her sprint.

"She has energy, that girl," Flo muttered.

Emma was almost there when a dark shape launched itself out from behind a tree in her path. Her shriek rang into the night. My heart raced but I froze.

Then I registered Emma's hysterical laughter as she melted to the grass, and the figure reached out to her, laughing too.

"I hate you!" Emma screeched. Flo and I caught up as Reese hauled her to standing.

"I'm so sorry," he said, gasping for air. "I couldn't resist."

Emma pressed away from him and dusted herself off. "I'm going to get you so bad. Just you wait."

"Yeah, yeah." Reese finally looked at Flo and I, as if only just realising we were there too. "How was work?"

"It was all right," Flo said with a shrug. "Nothing special."

Emma crunched across the tanbark to the swings. "I had this table of oldies that really didn't wanna leave," she said loudly. "I thought they might stay forever and die there, before they'd even tipped me."

"Wow." Reese snorted. "That's dark. Why are you so dark Emma?"

She clambered into the baby swing and pulled the chain across her lap—she really was a tiny thing. "Dark is my middle name."

"I thought it was Loral," said Reese.

"Oi!" Emma pointed an accusatory finger his way. "We don't speak of this."

"You're the one who brought it up man," he countered.

Flo nudged my elbow as they continued to bicker, offering me an eye roll I could only just detect in the pale light of that sole lamp.

"Emma mentioned Ray is your uncle?" It took me a moment to realise Reese was now addressing me. "Does that mean you get paid more than us?"

Flo gasped. "Reese!"

"It's a *joke*," he said. "But does it?"

I gave a short laugh, laced with an exceptional degree of discomfort. "It probably means I get paid less," I told him, which was likely to be true. Eighteen dollars an hour. I had less experience than the others, and with family ties came obligatory love jobs. I was surprised Mum let Uncle Ray pay me at all.

The sound of a car door had us all spinning to the road. Jesse's frame loped across the park toward us. I snuck a glance at Flo, who had shifted into her standard Jesse posture–stiff-backed and tight-lipped.

My mind went to the sketch I saw on her bedroom floor. It was Jesse all over. He was still on her mind enough to require escape onto paper. The thought made my heart ache for her, especially as Jesse joined the group and I caught a glimpse of the strain in Flo's smile.

"Oh, I thought it was the boogey man or something," Reese said, slapping Jesse on the back. "But this is heaps worse."

"Who invited the clown?" Jesse countered. His gaze skirted the group as he ran a hand through his hair. I hadn't seen it loose before, curling at the ends.

"My bad," Emma called from the swing.

Reese started chattering to Jesse about people I didn't know–who once worked at Corner, I assumed–as we all sauntered across to where Emma swung. I took a seat at a four-person see-saw nearby, followed by Flo who sat opposite. We kicked our heels into the ground and tipped up and down as the boys kept talking. That same, increasingly familiar rush of companionship bloomed in my chest. I was glad to act as somewhat of a buffer, if Flo was in fact feeling uncomfortable around

Jesse. She offered me a firm smile and wide eyes, that if I had to guess, said something to the effect of—*I feel awkward*.

Jesse left Reese and Emma—Reese was now pushing her way too high on the swing—and wandered over to the seesaw, stepping up onto its centre. "Hey how's the painting going? I've been meaning to ask ..."

"Oh." Flo let out a flat laugh. "Uh, well thanks. Yeah, pretty well."

She seemed so calm and collected, usually. So I was surprised to hear her stumbling over her words. I wondered if this was the first time they'd spoken since that awards night, where things turned sour.

"How about the photography?" she asked.

"Good, good." Jesse jumped off the seesaw and sat on one of the seats between us instead. It sunk to the ground on his side, lifting our feet off the bark. "Just been building up my portfolio for that interview with RMIT. Need to have something worthy to show."

"Nice. When is it?"

"In like a month," Jesse said through a sigh. "Hey, where's Darcy? He never turns down a group thing."

"He does if Nina wants him to," Emma interposed. "Okay, stop now, I'm getting dizzy." The swing jolted as Reese grabbed at its rubber ropes before Emma sprung out from them.

"We haven't done anything like this in ages," Jesse muttered. Flo glanced at me, only fleetingly, but enough for me to know the comment had triggered something. I decided I would ask her later how she felt. I got the impression she might want me to. But it seemed, like me, she would never admit to needing a listening ear.

Reese plunked himself down on the last remaining seat of the seesaw and Emma claimed the centre.

"I'm thinking house party this weekend," Reese declared. "The folks are jetting off to Brizzy to see fam, so … carpe diem."

"What the hell did you just say?" Emma twisted around to cast him a frown.

"Carpe diem," he repeated. "It's my mantra. *Seize the day*. *Make your lives extraordinary*. Dead Poet's Society?"

"I don't read," Emma drawled. "You know this."

Reese reached forward to shove her–she grabbed the post she was sitting on to keep balance. "It's a movie, dingus."

"Why don't you two just tie the knot?" mused Jesse. "You already argue like an old married couple. You're halfway there."

Emma hooted into the sky. "Can you imagine?"

"We'd probably murder each other man," Reese said.

"Out of love, though." Emma kissed the air between them.

"Anyway—" Reese pretended to catch the kiss and throw it aside. "My place. Sunday night."

"I'm working," Flo said. "I think Kerry is on too."

Reese snorted. "Oh I wouldn't invite Kerry anyway. She's too old."

"Who's Kerry?" I asked, and realised then that I hadn't said much since we'd been at the park. The sound of my voice felt stark and loud and made my heart beat faster.

"She's like fifty," Reese answered. "Works Sunday shifts."

"Ageist," Jesse cut in.

"Would you invite Georgia?" Emma posed.

Reese barked a laugh. "Hell no. Don't want her stealing my alcohol."

Ah, the vodka thief, I presumed. "What happened there?" I asked. "Is this the girl who was fired before me?"

"Uh-huh." Emma nodded while Reese burst into laughter.

"She was only there for a couple of months," he said. "Bit of a loose unit that Georgia. But Ray put her in her place. I was there when he found the footage, and man you should've seen his face. I thought he was gonna implode."

It was strange having these people talk about my uncle like they knew him, when I'd known him my whole life.

"Flo, just come to mine after work," Reese went on. "We'll save you a spritzer."

I stopped listening then. My focus was drawn to the seesaw and the four stems connecting us all. It drew me out of my body until I was looking down from above, entirely removed from the conversation.

Aside from the pale lamplight, it was dark. But the dark is different when you're not the only one in it. There's no terror there. No isolation. Because you know that no matter what monsters are hiding, waiting, you won't have to face them alone.

By the time I got to Reese's, I was practically hyper-ventilating. I sat in my car with my hands tight on the steering wheel, breathing hard and sweating bullets.

I knew Reese and Emma, I told myself. Not well, but well enough. Darcy might be there too–though that thought only seemed to heighten my stress levels.

Jesse. I could talk to Jesse. And Flo would arrive later. It would be okay. It would be okay.

When I told Mum I was going to a party with work friends, I'd literally seen her ears prick up before she had time to play it cool and act as though parties were a regular occurrence for me.

Sometimes I felt like being an only child was a curse, more than a blessing. Every pair of eyes was on me, always. I guess it would make a lot of people happy to occupy every ounce of attention from their parents, and I didn't want to seem ungrate-ful … but too often I wanted to shrink away from it. Throw a curtain between them and me so I could count my breaths without them listening.

I stared up at the house a moment longer and got as far as unbuckling my seatbelt, before I decided to ditch. Kramer was waiting for me at home and there were cuddles to be had.

I'd only just turned on the ignition again—when Jesse showed up in the car behind me. I fumbled with my pawpaw tube and quickly smeared some on my lips. Then, before I could overthink it any longer, I got out as if he'd caught me arriving, not leaving.

"Hey, Dot." He sauntered over in torn jeans and a loose tee, smiling his half smile. "You look nice. Cool stockings."

I swept a hand across my dress—a red number I'd paired with black stockings and doc martins—and swallowed a nervous laugh. "Thanks."

My fingers were tingling like firecrackers as we went to the door. Did everyone feel this jittery arriving at a party?

Everything I did was accompanied by an insidious, frantic buzz of nerves. All my words and movements bound themselves to the sound until it became white noise.

My anxiety rarely announced itself in full back then. I didn't know what to call it, or how to define it. It was a grey area. Everything inside your head was grey, really, because you were the only one that could exist there. And who's to say you were the most reliable source?

Reese welcomed us inside with enthusiastic embraces, where speakers blared R&B beats and various bottles were lined along a wide kitchen bench. There were at least two-dozen people scattered around on couches and stools, and some out by a brilliantly blue pool.

My gaze fell on Darcy—standing by the bench. I'd never seen him in casual clothes. Tonight he wore blue board shorts and a white tee shirt. There was something fascinating about seeing everyone *outside* of work for the first time. When we were all in uniform, fewer assumptions could be made. Now we were whatever we wanted to be.

What would people deduce from my outfit choice? The dress was a bit much compared to what everyone else was wearing, which was mostly jeans or shorts. I hoped it wouldn't give me the look of someone trying too hard. Nobody else was supposed to know I tried hard.

Darcy was twirling a spoon in a glass, mixing something orange and yellow. It was only when he passed the concoction off to a slim brunette that I noticed he wasn't alone. She took it and seemed to ask a question I couldn't decipher, until I saw Darcy scouring the bench and returning with a straw.

"Dot?"

I turned to see Jesse lifting an inquiring brow my way.

"Yeah?"

"I asked if you wanted a drink."

"Oh." I didn't dare cast another glance back at Darcy, for fear of Jesse realising where my attention had been–if he hadn't already. "No, I'm okay."

"I'll get you a drink," he said anyway. "You go find us a corner."

I wondered if he was saving me from having to speak to Darcy and the brunette I assumed was his girlfriend, Nina. Whether he could sense my discomfort.

Maybe that was giving him too much credit. In my experience, boys generally tended to exhibit a lower EQ than one expected. The other possibility of course was that I applied too much meaning to things, which was certainly valid too.

After a rapid scan of the room, I spotted a free couch by the TV and made for it like lightning. I dropped my car keys onto a nearby table, straightened the hem of my dress and crossed my legs. Then I uncrossed them, because maybe I looked too standoffish that way.

I tried not to look in Darcy's direction, and instead observed Reese on the opposite couch having an animated conversation with some dude who looked much like him–round glasses and hair styled in a wave.

Were guys involved in some low-key competition to see who could get their hair nearest the ceiling? Despite this pressing question, I couldn't stop my mind from travelling back to the kitchen. To the boy there whose hair wasn't some strange architectural feat–just a perfectly imperfect coiffe.

I wasn't sure why I felt so repelled by Darcy's companion. He had never expressed interest in me, and I hadn't expressed interest in him either. There was a good chance I was just lonely, searching for someone. Anyone. Seeing that picture of Cameron and his scantily dressed companion on Facebook was just nudging me towards the nearest male.

You've met other guys since Cameron, but no one like Darcy. I tried not to dwell on the thought.

You met Jesse around the same time, but you don't have feelings for him. That was true. But again, what was the point? Darcy was clearly off-limits.

I watched Jesse navigate his way to the couch, two bottles in hand. "Smirnoff Double Blacks," he declared, passing one over and sinking into the sliver of couch beside me. "Is that acceptable?"

"Sure." Some tiny burst of confidence made me clink my bottle against his before taking a sip. He looked surprised too.

"I know it's a girly drink, but I love it." Jesse's smile was an endearing combination of humour and relief, as if it were a bold admission he hadn't shared with many before me. "Tastes like lemonade."

He was right, it did. I didn't often drink and I'd never been drunk, but even I knew that alcohol that didn't taste like alcohol was dangerous territory.

"So tell me something we don't know about you," Jesse said. He was so close I could smell the sweetness of the Smirnoff on his breath. Immediately I thought of Flo, and shifted away a little.

I considered denying there was anything left to know about me, but that wasn't quite true. So I decided to try a little harder. "Okay. I like French films and novels with sad endings, and I collect business cards."

Jesse blinked at me, bottle pressed to his lips. "French, hey?" He smirked. "They can be quite … risqué, can't they?"

"Not all of them," I said quickly. But he was right. There seemed to be less restriction on how much butt or boob could be shown. It was the reason I never watched them in the lounge with my parents hanging around. Dad even got all red-faced when Sexyland ads came up on TV, so it was for the best.

I took another sip. "I like the passion of them. Everything is devastating, or extravagant. And it's nice …" to feel something without having to endure it myself, I wanted to add, but didn't. Jesse nodded like he knew the end of the sentence.

"I get it. So what's the story with the business cards then?"

"I've collected them since ever. I guess it's just a habit now."

Jesse lifted himself off the couch and dug around in his back pocket. He pulled out his wallet and tugged on a white card, passing it across to me. I ran my thumb over the embossed words.

JESSE MELROSE

Photographer | Melbourne

Film | Digital

His mobile and social media tags were printed on the reverse side. It was a clean design, edged in black.

"I have to get it redone," he said. "I've changed my Instagram name since, so yeah."

"I'm impressed." I pocketed the card. "You and Flo, with all your artistic pursuits …" I hesitated, hoping things wouldn't turn awkward with my mention of Flo—but Jesse didn't seem bothered. "It's really admirable," I finished. "Full credit to you. How could RMIT turn down someone with a business card?"

"My plan exactly." Jesse grinned, but it faded quickly. "There's a good chance I won't get accepted though." He picked at the label of his bottle. It was the closest to nervous I'd seen him. "They have limited spots."

I swigged my liquid courage and shrugged. "Doesn't matter, though. It's the pursuit that counts.

You could even start up your own business, if all else fails."

Oh boy. I could hear Dad's voice in my own. He was always saying that one door doesn't close without another opening. There are pathways in all sorts of directions, each filled with entirely different joys and trials and successes. There is no *right* door. Because what you might consider a loss behind one could be a gain behind another.

I liked that. It was one of those annoying *glass half-full* mentalities, but a worthy one that I could get on board with most of the time.

Just as I went to tell Jesse about it, Darcy came around the couch to hand Reese a bottle of water. When he looked up our eyes met. His smile was rapid and a little awkward, but it made my heart skitter.

He cut a glance to Jesse and his expression slipped a touch–into what, I wasn't sure–but Jesse waved him over and his smile returned.

"Hey." He stopped in front of us, hands on his hips. "The whole crew's here. Reese knows how to host a last minute gath." His eyes dropped to my drink. I hadn't realised how fast I'd drunk it. There was barely any left. I curled my hand around the bottle to hide the fact.

"What's up?" Darcy looked between us, his dark eyes glinting blue from the pool's light outside.

"Just chatting," Jesse answered. "Did you lose Nina?"

"Uh–" Darcy twisted, searching the room. "Nah, nah. She's still here. Did you bring bathers? Either of you?"

I shook my head as Jesse chuckled. "Reese's pool isn't heated," he said.

Darcy groaned. "He told me it was."

Jesse drained the last of his Smirnoff and said, "He lied," then tucked the bottle into the couch. "You know better than to believe anything Reese says."

"Compulsive liar?" I interposed. It would be an unsurprising revelation, if it were true. Reese was one of those people my nerves didn't appreciate– wild and carefree, often to the point of excess.

"At least one lie in every bloody conversation." Jesse shook his head. "You'll learn to pick them."

Darcy swore under his breath, chewing his lip as he stared at the pool through the window behind us. The gesture drew my attention to the fact that I was gnawing through mine too.

A hand slunk around Darcy's arm, followed by the same pretty brunette from before. "Oh, there you are," he said, swinging his arm around her. "You've met Jesse." He nodded to me. "This is Dot. Her Uncle owns Corner. You know Ray?"

"Cool," Nina said. She looked at me with about as much interest as I would give my finance notes.

Then she pressed her lips to Darcy's ear. "Can we get going soon?"

I cut my gaze to the floor as Darcy told her they hadn't even been there an hour, and as she huffed and told him she had an early rise the next day, and as he said they'd leave soon. Feeling suitably awkward, I put my drink to my lips and tipped it until only a drop reached my tongue.

Eventually, Nina managed to convince Darcy to go outside and dragged him away.

"She's a piece of work," Jesse muttered, grabbing his empty bottle and knocking it against his knuckles. I cut him a questioning look. "Darc is the good guy that gets stomped all over," he elaborated. "Nina says jump and he does a forward somersault on concrete."

I recalled Flo saying something similar.

"But anyway, what were we talking about before? Oh!" He tapped my knee with his bottle. "You were agreeing to model for me."

I laughed—then stopped short. "What?" If it was a joke, I didn't get it.

"I need more photos for my portfolio, and you'd be perfect for it." His smile sloped sideways. "You in?"

"Uh, not so much." All our family photos over the years flashed before my eyes. I had a photo face, and it was atrocious. My cousin Peter liked to point it out at every event, zooming in on me only to laugh and say things like—*were you in physical pain when this was taken?* Or … *looks like you just peed your pants* before proceeding to coax a *normal smile* out of me.

Maybe it was the Double Black talking, but I decided to say, "Flo would be better, you should ask her."

Jesse's brows rose high. "You bring her up a lot."

"No I don't."

He wasn't fooled. "Do you want to know more about all that?"

I shrugged, torn between *yes* and *I'd rather not— because then I'll have to decide whether to tell Flo or keep it from her.* I was betraying somebody's trust either way.

Jesse went on before I could tell him not to. "We hooked up once, after the last awards night." Well I knew that much. "I really liked her. Like, a lot. But then, I don't know … it didn't go anywhere. I was dealing with a whole lot of shit at the time and I didn't want to drag someone else through it."

I bit down on the urge to ask for more, hoping he'd get to it himself.

"Have you seen her paintings?" he asked, eyes wider now. They were a strange colour—a cerulean blue flecked with lighter streaks, like ice melting across the ocean.

"Yeah, I have."

"They're actually incredible." He sat back, knocking the glass bottle against his leg in time with the music. "She doesn't know I've seen them, though. I found her website online."

"I don't get it. If you both like each other, what's the issue?"

"If you go grab me another one of these, I might tell you." He poked me again with the end of his Double Black. I swiped it and craned my neck to see the kitchen. Only a couple of people loitered there, so I seized my opportunity and made my way over.

The room lost focus a little–confirmation of my lightweight status. It was probably a good thing I didn't particularly like alcohol. With my degree of social anxiety I'd probably become one of those people who never left the house without a flask in their pocket.

I found the Double Blacks in an esky on the bench and took two, deciding to pace myself with the second. When I turned back around I stumbled right into a sodden Emma. She was shivering and wrapped in a towel. "It's freezing," she said, her teeth clacking together. "Freaking Reese. I go to feel the temperature and he pushes me in–clothes and phone and all! Lucky it's waterproof, the idiot."

"That sounds … unpleasant."

"Can confirm," she replied, grimacing over her shoulder. "Is Flo here?" I shook my head as Emma eyed the drinks I was carrying. "Who's that for then?"

I hesitated a moment before answering, "Jesse."

"Oh." Emma gave me a funny look. "I feel like I should say … just, be careful. You know Flo was keen on him, don't you? Probably still is." If I hadn't known already, it wasn't a very discreet way of informing me. I got the sense Emma was often like that—brash and unapologetic about things others might say in a hush.

After brushing her warning aside with a rapid series of reassurances, I felt hugely conspicuous walking back to Jesse. Darcy was standing with Nina by the pool outside. I might've only imagined it, but I was fairly sure he was looking my way.

Jesse took the drink and gave me a nod, smiling and taking a swig.

"So." I dropped back into the couch and tried to ignore Emma's words of caution, which were repeating themselves in my head over and over. "Feel free to share."

My bubbly, vodka-infused brain didn't quite recall what Jesse had agreed to share in exchange for the drink, but he clearly did. Because he sat forward and said, "Flo's someone who has all her shit together. She's everything you think she is, you know? Attractive, composed, driven … I didn't want to wreck that vibe."

"Nobody is everything you think they are," I said.

"Well then she's the exception." Jesse paused. Smacked his lips together. "I told you a while ago that I have a little sister. But I don't. Minty died from leukaemia last year, right after her ninth birthday."

I was lost for anything suitable to say. Silence seemed the only answer, so I just waited. His eyes flickered away from mine.

"Her name was Miriam, but I called her Minty because Miriam sounded too … old and boring, for who she was."

I wanted to ask why he was telling me this, and how it related to Flo. But then, I could guess the answer to both. He didn't tell Flo because in his eyes, she was too perfect and unblemished to burden, and he could tell me because I wasn't either of those things. Well, as far as he knew I could be anything. He needed to tell someone, and I was the nearest blank slate.

"I'm so sorry," I said, training my voice into something soft enough to sound sincere, but not so soft that it might crumble into pity.

Jesse shrugged. "It is what it is."

I remembered then that he had told me about his sister once before—back when we went for kebabs with Darcy after my first shift. He had spoken of her like she was still around. And so I wondered …

"Does Darcy know?"

Jesse shook his head. "No one at Corner knows."

I swallowed hard, taking that in.

"So there's been a lot to deal with at home," he continued. "Parents separating and all. And I guess I wasn't ready to let Flo in on that. To let anyone in on it."

The music pounded and swirled around us, but we were encased in a bubble that sent all other noise into an insignificant outer space. Everything was muffled except Jesse's voice and my heart was beating fast–maybe from the pressure of knowing his secret, or from an aching sympathy, or not knowing what to say next.

My eyes became trapped in his for a moment. Without that drink to calm my jitteriness, I might've looked away. But I held it, beyond what was comfortable, because there was no comfort in what he'd told me. And nothing romantic in the gaze. Something sharp and hard connected us in those few seconds, maybe an unspoken understanding, or an acknowledgement of a milestone he'd inadvertently passed.

Only when I finally looked away did I see Flo. She was leaning against the far wall still wearing her work shirt over jeans and speaking to Reese. Well, he was speaking to her, hands accompanying his animated storytelling, while she watched me and Jesse.

Seeming to register my attention shift, Flo cut her own attention back to Reese. But her eyes were a little too blank; her mouth turned into a wonky smile that I didn't buy for a second.

She had seen me gazing into the eyes of the boy she adored. How must it have looked? We were sitting close together too, sipping on Smirnoff Blacks. I scooted closer to the couch's edge.

"You can tell her," Jesse said. "If you want."

He was observing me observing Flo, and bemusement drew his expression into one that didn't match the importance of what he'd said. Once again I was poised between him and her, given information from one to tell the other. But this was different. His little sister was dead, and I was the only one who knew. I had to be sure he really wanted it shared.

"You really want her to know?" I asked straight out. "For sure?"

He leaned back and shrugged, setting his eyes on her. By the time he returned them to me, a realisation had dawned there. "Yeah, I do."

Before I left that night, I unscrewed the lid of my empty bottle and held onto it till I got to my car. My memento shelf was full of useless crap, but I wanted to remember this night for the boy who had chosen me to confide in first.

JESSE

I'm not sure what compelled me to say it, but I'd learnt not to question myself too much. I did whatever felt right to do. Generally what felt right–was right. And if it was wrong, there was a good chance I needed to get it out of my system anyway.

Doctor Jenson had always said talking about Minty was essential. That it would keep her memory alive. Honestly, I hadn't really taken his advice on board. Mum and I spoke about her, yeah, but no one else knew Minty like we did, so they wouldn't understand what it meant that she was gone. Even Dad dismissed the topic because it made him watery-eyed and awkward.

Telling Dot about Minty was a surprise even to me. But it felt right, so I did it. Dot was private. There were walls around her. No doubt they were for her own protection, but I got the sense they could protect me too.

Driving home from Reese's, I thought the conversation over. I wondered when Dot would tell Flo, or if she would at all. They seemed close enough.

A few months ago, having Flo find out seemed like the worst idea ever. I never let on how bad things were. My anger. Guilt. I kept it all to myself and learned to maintain the steady hint of a smile most of the time so no one could pick up on how I really felt. Corner had become the place where Minty was still alive. The place where I still had a little sister.

Maybe the delusion was fading, or I was just realising that practically–I couldn't maintain it forever. The other possibility was that I missed Flo. That I was ready for her now, in a way I wasn't then. I couldn't expect her to bounce back to me but I could at least let her know why things hadn't worked out the first time. Well, Dot could …

Okay, I was a bloody chicken. But how do you tell someone that the sister you've been talking about for a year doesn't exist anymore?

When I got home from Reese's Dad was at the kitchen table hunched over paperwork. He only looked up when I chucked my keys on the table, and even then, barely.

"Hey," I said.

"Hi Jesse, how you going?"

He said that all the time. *How you going?* It ran off the end of his hellos but never sounded genuine.

And it wasn't really a question because I knew he never wanted an answer. He had too much going on to care.

Dad's landscape company went broke last week and everyone there was left jobless. The last few days had involved frantic calculations of our savings and applications submitted all over the place. I even heard him telling his friend over the phone that he'd applied for a management position at the supermarket.

They were separated now, Mum and Dad, but neither of them could afford to move out. So they just avoided each other like the plague.

Our fridge was still covered in photos of Minty. Baring her teeth, or lack of–the front two missing, sitting on my knee wearing elf ears two Christmas's ago, kissing Mum's cheek with her eyes pinched shut, grinning over a Freddo cake in a paper crown. I swung the fridge open and took a swig of orange juice straight from the bottle. Then I went to my room and closed the door.

It was a bit of a rubbish tip, but I liked it that way. I never trusted people with spotless bedrooms. They were overcompensating, lying to themselves. Nobody had their shit together, so why pretend?

That is, nobody except Flo. She was as close to perfect as I'd ever come to seeing. After the awards night I invited her over on some senseless impulse. She'd stepped into my room and her eyebrows went way up as she scanned the mess. I was quick to turn the light off and guide her to my bed. In the dark, there could be no judgment.

I didn't tell her about Minty, even then. Even when she asked if my little sister was home. Even when we tiptoed to the front door past Minty's room, where Minty wasn't sleeping, and I held my finger to my lips as if she was.

And when she'd texted me the next morning asking to hang out again, I couldn't do it. The light of day changed things. I was Jesse Melrose, the boy who'd lost his sister to leukaemia and sunk into the darkest sort of depression in her absence, the boy who was ignored by his separated parents, the boy who took photos of beautiful things mostly just to remind himself there was a reason to stay in a world that Minty Melrose was no longer a part of.

I was a boy who was no match for the beautiful, elusive Florence Morgan. What a name, too. I always thought it suited her.

Working shifts with Flo was practically torture. She looked at me differently now, with this cold, hard expression, if she looked my way at all.

I should never have asked her home that night. Not that it wasn't amazing, it's just–*nothing* would be worth hurting Florence Morgan for. At least with Dot in the know, Flo might find out why it came to a crashing halt as soon as it had begun. There was some relief in that, even if nothing came of it.

Since Minty died, I didn't care about much, least of all myself. But I felt that starting to change. I was nervous about what Flo might think of me. I was getting nervous about that RMIT interview. And nerves meant caring.

I crossed to my desk and flipped through my portfolio, the couple of pages I put together yesterday. A sunset down at Rye—long exposure turning the sea into a blanket that covered the sand around clusters of jagged rock. A cityscape dotted with colourful hot air balloons. The photos were solid, but the book wasn't finished. I needed at least a dozen more pages if I wanted them to take me seriously.

I smiled, recalling Dot's expression when I asked her to model for me. She'd do a bloody good job. She had this odd, pixie vibe—cropped hair and a sharp chin, and eyes that burned through you when they were brave enough to look. Maybe I told her about Minty for that reason. Because having her full attention felt like a privilege, as if you owed her something in return.

It was a Saturday and I was on with Darcy, as per usual. Flo had been different that week. She was polite whenever I dumped dishes in the kitchen, but hadn't gone out of her way to see me.

It *had* to be because of Reese's party. She was upset I'd been there with Jesse, or she was waiting for me to explain it. And I would. Jesse had granted me permission, in his own way. But what happened to his little sister still felt a strange story to pull out of nowhere, and definitely not one to share during work.

After our last few shifts Flo had left immediately after finishing, so I was coming to see that I was the one who would have to propose a time to catch up.

I hadn't arranged any sort of outing with a friend since high school. Even then I preferred to be asked, rather than the one asking. I didn't know why I was that way. Things that came naturally to most people often felt like trying to squeeze water out of a rock for me.

It wasn't only Flo who changed though—Darcy had, too. He was different that night, a little less chatty at the stand and looking my way every time he thought I wouldn't notice. We were closing the restaurant together, which meant we'd be the latest to stay.

Corner was hectic, but I managed to stay on top of all my orders without a single mishap. It was easy to glide between the tables now, knowing what to do and where everything was. I still dreaded approaching new customers and yelling *corner* entering the kitchen, but not in that knee-trembling, lip-gnawing way I did at the start.

There was a rhythm and a flow to taking orders, pouring drinks, serving dishes, clearing tables—a revolving fluency I came to enjoy, the more I became a seamless part of it.

Once the final customer left, Darcy and I started wiping down tables. He disappeared for a moment and the generic radio music Uncle Ray had going in the place was suddenly replaced by a loud rock tune. Darcy came out again, smiling at me and strumming an air guitar. "Jude lets you connect your phone to the speakers if he's in a good mood."

I grinned back at him as he laid the guitar down to tie a knot in the bin bag. Flo appeared behind him with her backpack. She was leaving, again. Without having spoken more than a few words to me.

"See you later guys." She swept by without much more than a glance in my direction, and my heart sank, because I knew I'd missed another opportunity to explain myself.

I dropped my tea towel to drag my hair back into control. It always sprung out of its ponytail during shifts. Darcy moved past me, swinging the rubbish bag as he went.

"Come with me," he said over his shoulder. "I'll show you where the bins are."

I followed him out the back door beside the bar into an alleyway, where further along the bins were pressed against a brick wall.

The smell was less than ideal.

"I know," he said, probably registering my crinkled nose. "It's disgusting." He swung the bag up and over the nearest bin's edge. "Reese told me he saw a possum family living in here once. He says a lot of shit but that was probably true."

"Well, Uncle Ray always calls Corner a family restaurant," I told him. "Who are we to discriminate against possums?"

Darcy wiped his hands on his apron. "Too true, too true."

Silence grew in the space between us, broken only by wheels on asphalt from the main road. Darcy tipped his head back at the sky. His hair fell away from his face and jaw, revealing lines I'd never seen. "You ever been to the country?"

"Uh, Mum and Dad took me to a caravan park in Daylesford ages back," I said, already picking up where the question might lead. "There are so many stars out there, is that what you were thinking? I mean, stars you can actually see."

Darcy nodded and looked at me, his hair falling a little over an eye. "There's so much you can't see here, but it still exists," he said. "Just, somewhere else. And you'll never know how it looks unless you go there. Isn't that weird?"

I was frantically reaching for a double meaning— certain there was one. Only I had no idea what it was. Maybe he really was just talking about the stars.

———◆———

You never think it will be you until it is. There was so little distance to cross. The length of a swimming pool, if that. It only took an instant for one life to collide with another. That was the problem.

Jude called Darcy into his office once everything was packed up to discuss the roster, so I scanned my fingerprint and bid them farewell. I didn't want to linger. Didn't want Darcy to think I was waiting around for him. He had a Nina, I reminded myself. Whatever that talk of the stars was about, I had no right to dwell on it. And then I was mad, because he had no right to give me something to dwell on.

I shrugged my bag up over my shoulder and pulled my keys out as I ambled across the Corner car park. There were only a few cars left and no one else in sight. A nervous jolt whittled through me—the silence and dark enough to trigger my panic.

I should have run the rest of the way. I'd done it before on those rare occasions I'd been out and about late at night, on my own. But this time I didn't, because a part of me thought Darcy might see me and think I was a wimp.

That would've been preferable to what really happened, in hindsight. But hindsight is never kind, or forgiving.

As I approached my car, I pressed unlock and it blinked hello. That's when I caught glimpse of a shape in my side vision, appearing from behind a silver car to my left.

It didn't happen the way you see in films—a gun pulled and held to the victim's head as money is demanded and time is allowed to get it out.

No. This was a rapid, fumbling collision. A muffled demand and a sharp edge against my throat. No time to think.

It was my hands shaking, my heart rushing into panic, the sound of ragged breaths. Mine, maybe his. And in the moment I finally managed to unzip my bag and throw my purse—a hard shove that sent me smacking against the concrete. Wheels screeching sharply into the night as I lay very still where I'd fallen, unable to move.

It was fast. Too fast for what it did to me.

15

You might think it was silly—people get robbed all the time. And sure, they do. But too often split-second events are deemed trivial. Insignificant. As if the time they stole from us should indicate the time it will take to move past them.

I wish that were true.

It took a few minutes to gather myself. To understand what exactly had happened. The damage of the fall was mostly to my hands, which were all cut up and speckled red, my wrists sore and elbows stinging.

The world was fuzzy and rapidly closing in on me while I fumbled for my bag, my keys, clambered into the nearest back seat of my car and locked the doors. Even then everything continued to contract; my chest, my breaths, the space in the car. I felt faint and disconnected.

A rap on glass had me flinging myself across the back seat. Away. Away.

"Dot?" Darcy's face slid into view as he ducked to see in the window. His voice was muffled, like my thoughts and everything else. "You all right? What the–" His expression shifted from mild concern to a darker alertness. "What happened?"

My teeth were locked over any possibility of words. Unyielding. I just shook my head.

"Dorothy." He was firmer now, and I couldn't recall any other time he'd called me by my full name. I almost wanted to laugh. "Can you open the door?"

I willed myself to speak but still couldn't manage so much as a gasp. Without thinking too much, I unlocked the car and attempted to steady my breathing through my teeth as Darcy dropped into the back seat beside me.

"Shit … did you fall?" Darcy leaned forward, resting his temple against the front seat. "You're bleeding."

He couldn't see my hands–they were pressed against my pants, the raw skin hidden. I glanced at him and noted the line of his gaze. My fingers reached up to my neck and although I couldn't feel much, they came away sticky and crimson. It was only as I inspected them that I realised how much I was shaking.

Then I remembered the sharpness against my throat. A knife. It must have been a knife.

"Dot." Darcy laid a light hand on my knee. "What the hell happened?"

After a length of silence, during which I tried to make sense of it all myself, I finally found my voice. "This guy–he came out of nowhere and just, I don't know. Asked for my purse. And I—I gave it and he had a knife I think." My voice was trembling more than my body. "I think he pushed me and I hit the ground, pretty hard. And then he took off."

Darcy looked so stricken the colour seemed to drain from his face right before my eyes. He started muttering and got out of the car, circling it once, then twice, as if the perpetrator might have decided to hide underneath it. Then he clambered back inside and pulled out his mobile.

"What are you doing?"

"Calling the police." Darcy frowned at my neck. "Then we'll get you cleaned up." I knew he was right to call, but the thought still sent a jolt of panic through me. I barely listened to what he said over the phone, but I registered the stilted way he spoke. He seemed nervous too.

Then he passed it on to me.

A woman with a steady voice asked a few basic questions about my location and how it all happened, and then a few detailed ones, like *can you tell me what he was wearing? Which direction did you see his car go?* I couldn't answer much of the latter. I didn't know. Or maybe shock had blotted out those parts.

Darcy watched me carefully as I spoke, his brow knotted the entire time. It was strange, having him there. I wasn't sure if I was grateful or embarrassed for him to see me this way. But if he hadn't, I might've spent the whole night hyperventilating in my car. So, I supposed it was a good thing.

The policewoman told me there would be someone at the car park soon, and to stay calm and lock the doors. Darcy locked them, so he must have been able to hear her too.

When the call ended I envisaged sirens and cars tearing toward us at top speed, and my heart rate reached new heights.

"You got band-aids or something anywhere here?" Darcy asked.

"Uh …" I reached for the middle console, digging around inside—palms burning—until I found my little emergency kit. Mum gave it to me years back, when we first bought the car. It was a small purse with polka-dots. She claimed that every car should have something similar. This was the first time I was opening it.

There were tweezers, nail scissors, tissues, a bandage and band-aids. Darcy rifled through it, pulling a few things out. "I don't really know how this works," he said, unravelling the bandage.

"Geez, what are you planning to do with that?" Despite the gravity of the situation, a laugh burst from me. "It's just a cut."

Darcy continued to wrestle with the bandage. "Dot, you're bleeding out on the seat."

I couldn't stop the laughter then, even though it was borderline maniacal and Darcy wasn't joining in. He shifted to face me and wrapped the bandage around my neck. Once. Twice.

"Are you trying to strangle me?" I was gasping for air, partially from the pressure but mostly from the laughter.

"This can't be right," Darcy muttered, his frown deepening.

"The police will be here soon," I said. "They might think you're trying to finish the job."

"Oh Lord, don't say that." A smile snuck into the corner of his mouth. He blinked a few times as if that would send it away, but it grew the more I laughed. "Shit, Dot. This is bad."

I pulled the crimson-stained bandage off my neck and swiped a band-aid from his hand, fiddling with the wrapper. I was still shaking, and after two failed attempts to get it out, Darcy snatched it from me.

"Let me." So I let him. It might have been a pleasant moment if I wasn't crying and laughing at the same time. He pressed five band-aids to my neck and then turned my hands over, adding another three to the worst of the cuts there.

My sobbing hysterics eased, and Darcy drew his hands away sharply the moment the band-aids were in place–like my skin was suddenly scorching to the touch. I figured it was probably his skin that burnt. That second layer that wasn't mine or anyone else's, but Nina's. A coating around every bit of him that was hers alone. The thought sparked a flicker of envy somewhere deep inside me and I imagined–perhaps due to my delirious state of mind–pulling that layer away just enough to take his hand.

Darcy sighed, but it came out as more of a frustrated exclamation and made me wonder what *he'd* been thinking about.

"I should've walked you out," he said, in a voice racked with so much guilt I was actually startled to hear it. I shook my head, too fast. The base of my neck throbbed.

"Don't be silly." I shut my eyes, attempting to block out the ache. "How could you have known?"

Darcy cast me a wary look, and I knew he wasn't at all reassured. And really, it was a stupid question anyway. *How could you have known?* Sure, it was true. But truth was rarely comforting, and rarely what you needed to hear.

I touched the row of band-aids under my jaw and considered telling him instead–*it could be worse*. But I never got to, because a flashing police car and ambulance wheeled into the car park and we stepped out into the starless night.

16

Darcy agreed to keep the attack under wraps for the time being. I felt conspicuous already being relatively new to Corner, and I didn't want to be known forever as that girl who was robbed in the car park. I didn't want to remember it at all, or especially be the subject of pity because of it. I was already a sad case. It would only make me seem sadder.

I even considered hiding it from Mum and Dad, so as not to worry them. But when I came in the front door and they looked up from their books on the couch, their faces dropped, and I started to bawl.

The inner child in me must have desperately needed a hug. I got it, tucked into the couch between them as they patted my back with eyes wider than small planets, but I also received another interrogation that probably rivalled the police's.

I didn't say much about Darcy—only that a coworker had come by my car right after the guy took off and had helped me call the police.

"Was it that young Liam Neeson?" Dad asked.

"*Jim*," Mum snapped over my head.

"What? It's a simple question."

"Yeah, Dad." I still had strength enough to roll my eyes. "It was Liam Neeson."

Once they were both satisfied I'd done all I could, Mum stripped off the thick dressing the ambos had adorned me with to check the wound herself. Her face went white and I averted my eyes. Then she checked me over, head to toe, and told me I'd be okay.

"We should tell Ray," Dad said, tapping on his phone screen with one pointed, trembling finger. "Can't have people like this hanging around Corner. He'll be furious."

"Dad–" I wanted to say *don't tell Ray*, but that sounded ridiculous. And there's no way I could convince Mum or Dad to keep it from him. So instead I said, "Tell him not to spread it around."

Dad glanced at Mum–then back at me. "As far as I'm concerned, everyone should be told," he said. "What if this moron comes back?"

"Please," I whispered, more than said. Dad frowned but said nothing as he continued on his phone, while Mum stroked my hair.

That night, I didn't feel alone in the dark of my room. I stayed wide-awake with the covers pulled up over my mouth while every shadow made itself known. Shadows that moved when I looked away and loomed when I gave them my attention. Even the carpet seemed to make noises I'd never heard before.

Funny how the places you loved could turn on you. How what happened one night could transform a room and have it looking entirely different the next.

———•——

To him, I was a stranger. And he should've been the same to me. But he wasn't. He would become everything. An empty car park, a crowd, night descending, and the morning I couldn't meet without flinching. He was faceless, but he was every face.

It took a bit of to-ing and fro-ing, but eventually Mum and Dad agreed to let me continue at Corner–under the proviso that Mum would drive me there and pick me up. She claimed it was just until the police had more information on the attack.

I didn't point out that there was still a chance we would never know who the guy actually was, and she couldn't drive me everywhere for the rest of my life. But I let her take me anyway, partially because the idea of being alone in that car park again scared the crap out of me and also to ease her nerves, which–if you can believe–sometimes ran faster than mine.

The cut on my neck was starting to scab over. I peeled the tape off as soon as I could. I decided the best way to deal with what happened, was to pretend it didn't. So I avoided looking in the mirror.

After answering more questions down at the police station, I boxed up that entire night, taped up every edge and didn't look at it again. It worked during the day, but when the sun fell, I fell with it.

Uncle Ray was waiting for me outside Corner before my next shift. He folded his arms and ducked his head to my level. "Any more news?"

"No."

"Ah, I still can't believe it. Are you feeling okay today? Coming back?"

I nodded, adjusting my high fashion neck scarf that had me looking like a 1950's airline hostess. "Mhm." *Stop talking about it.*

"You know, sometimes life throws us curveballs, girl. Whopping big ones that knock us down too easily." A distant glaze came over his eyes. I recognised it. It was the look he gave whenever he spoke about Aunty Rhea leaving. "But, there's nothing else to do but carry on. Get on with things despite the setbacks. So, I'm proud of you." He returned to his eyes, their corners crinkling. "You're an absolute trooper and the crew misses you."

I didn't want to talk about me anymore, and he seemed to register it—because he clapped my back and swept me inside before he left.

I told myself to ignore the thumping of my heart as I stepped into the back office and pulled my apron tight around my waist, like the straps alone could hold me together.

Jesse was working out the front with me, while Emma made coffees in the kitchen. At first, everything was manageable. My smile was surface-level but I kept it there, barely afloat whenever

I approached tables or laughed at Emma's jokes. It was only when I served a solitary teen in a grey hoodie that the unwelcome thoughts started creeping in.

The poor guy was probably entirely innocent, but I found myself wondering why he was alone. And I started thinking that maybe my attacker had been watching me. That maybe he had been a customer too, or at least knew when I'd be leaving the restaurant. I imagined eyes outside the window. Following me back and forth.

But I kept breathing. Slow ins. Slower outs. Restricted my wandering mind to the length of my arms. Taking glassware from the dishwasher. Wiping down the stand. Replacing cutlery. I'd steadied myself relatively well, at least I thought I had—until Jesse stepped in front of me at the stand and made me jump.

"What's going on?" he said. "You seem strange tonight."

"Strange? No, not at all." I tapped an order into the screen from my notepad, refusing to look at him in case my eyes gave it all away.

Jesse drummed his fingers against the screen's edge. "If this is about what I told you at Reese's, you really shouldn't–"

"Oh–no. Of course it isn't." I cut my gaze to him. I'd almost forgotten what he told me about his little sister, Minty. A flush of shame coloured my cheeks.

It was a huge admission, one he hadn't shared with anybody else at Corner. I wouldn't want him to think I'd taken it lightly. "It's nothing to do with that."

"Then what is it?"

I blinked at the screen as if it might supply me with some believable excuse if I concentrated on it hard enough, or explode to create a distraction whereby Jesse would drop the subject.

"Don't toy with me Dot." He narrowed his eyes, and then pointed to my scarf. "What's with the new look?"

I'd so intentionally chosen to ignore the cut on my neck that it took me a moment to remember why I was wearing a scarf at all. For a moment, I was stumped.

Jesse could see that I'd changed, which, oddly enough, was nice to hear. It meant he *knew* me in some sort of consistent, reliable sense. Knew me enough to know when I wasn't fully *me*. And that made me want to tell him exactly what was different. I *wanted* to.

But I couldn't. Even though Jesse had confided in me, I couldn't summon the courage to confide in him. The box was wrapped up too tight. I wasn't sure what would happen if I opened it.

So I said, "Just trying something different," and kicked that smile back upright. "I'm fine. Promise." I pressed through the final order and spun away from the stand, fairly certain he was still watching me.

Jesse and I had finished our close, but Mum was only just leaving home. I took a seat nearby the door to wait for her. Jesse was still chatting to Jude in the office, but I hoped one or both of them would stay at least until she arrived. I didn't want to brave that car park alone. Without any distractions, it would be harder to keep a lid on the box. To keep everything in.

Jesse sauntered out from the back, shrugging his backpack higher up his shoulder. I was considering how to ask if he would wait with me when he said, "Slurpee run?"

"What?"

"That 7-Eleven in the next block." He dragged his hair into a bun and inclined his head toward the main road. "Want to go?"

I chewed my lip, peering outside the window. It was almost eleven, so there wouldn't be many people around. Safer to go home.

But then, if I was supposed to be acting like nothing had changed, how was this different from going to Marley Park? I wasn't alone. Jesse was here. It was only a block away.

They haven't caught the guy. What if he's still around?

"Mum's already left," I tried. "My car is … she's had to drive me recently. So maybe next time."

"Ah, come on!" Jesse nudged my shoulder. "We'll be quick. What's that thing Reese is always saying? Carpe something …"

Reluctantly, I offered, "Carpe diem."

"Carpe bloody diem. Let's go–I need my sugar hit." Jesse jiggled on the spot while I checked my phone. If Mum left when she texted, I had about ten minutes.

It was only when Jesse started to frown that I found myself nodding. The best way to prove I was okay was to act like I was okay.

We walked around Corner and back up along the street, past Tommy's Kebabs. My heart thudded against the wall of my chest and got faster with the appearance of every stranger we passed. Especially those walking alone. But there weren't many of them, and Jesse did a fairly good job of distracting me in between times.

Most of the way we argued about slurpee flavours, which started because he had the nerve to declare cola inferior to the rest. I couldn't let that slide. I was a cola snob through and through, whereas Jesse preferred the sweeter flavours that turned your tongue blue or pink or orange. When I pointed out the colour factor, he declared that was only another reason to choose them.

"The sweeter, the better," he said. "Choosing cola is like … eating a pancake without the maple syrup."

"Cola is classic," I said. "People who stray from it can't be trusted."

Jesse laughed—a high-pitched, goofy sound. "I'm very trustworthy."

I puckered my lips, skating my eyes across his inquiring gaze and glinting studs—then shrugged the subject away.

"So you've been at Corner for three years, right?" I said. "Do you plan on staying there forever?"

"Oh yeah, isn't that everyone's dream? Running food and cleaning out dirt from old dishwashers—it's the best."

"So not so much, then."

"I take photos," he said. "That's what I want to pursue once I've got the money to back myself as a struggling artist." Jesse lifted his hands in a square, as if framing the street for a shot. "My parents might help out a bit, but I want to pay my own way through the course."

"That's really cool," I told him, honestly. "You look like the photographer type."

"You think?" He swept a hand through his messy hair and grinned, like it was a huge compliment.

At the door to 7-Eleven we stepped aside for a man carrying a takeaway coffee. I held my breath as he passed us.

Could've been him. You wouldn't know.

I squeezed my eyes shut a moment as if it would assist in resealing that box of unhelpful questions.

Then I drew a sharp breath to centre myself and moved into the store. If Jesse noticed the lapse, he didn't comment on it.

When we got to the slurpee machine I reached for the smallest cup. Jesse swiped it from me and tossed it in the nearby bin, grabbing two jumbo-sized cups instead.

I knew I'd never drink it all but I didn't argue, because he looked so pleased with himself. He shook his head at me as I filled mine to the brim with cola alone, while he went for a layered concoction of all the sherbety, wild and rainbow-coloured flavours on tap. Jesse paid for both despite my objections.

"That's just disgraceful," he told me as we left, shaking his head at my slurpee. "Try some of this."

I took his cup and gave it a sip. "Tastes like … redskins," I decided, smacking my lips together. "Or wizz fizz."

"I know." We switched back. "That's why it's so bloody good."

After a short silence, I remembered there was something I should probably address, and not many opportunities to get Jesse alone to say it.

"Hey," I started, hoping I sounded casual enough, "I haven't had a chance to talk to Flo yet. About what you told me."

"It's all good." Jesse whirled his straw around to mix his slurpee. "It isn't urgent or anything."

From across the road, two people were moving toward us. The closer they got, the more my body reacted. Fast heart. Clammy hands.

Why are they crossing here? To intercept us?

"The thing is," Jesse started, although I was only half-aware, "Flo and I were pretty close for a while, but it's been so long since we've spoken properly. And that's my fault."

I clutched onto my slurpee, imagining what might happen if I were to throw it at the approaching pair.

They stepped onto the pavement and the streetlight lit the faces of a guy and a girl walking arm-in-arm. I commanded myself to loosen my grip on my cup and focus on Jesse.

"I almost would've told her about Minty," he was saying. "Just, every opportunity slipped by, and then it was too late."

"Is it that you didn't want her feeling sorry for you?"

Jesse spooned ice onto his tongue, which was already turning a shocking shade of blue. "Partially. Sympathy is pointless and we copped a lot of it when she died. So yeah, maybe I didn't want to open that can of worms with Flo."

I sucked slurpee up my straw until I started to feel a brain freeze coming on. Hopefully it would numb my senses by the time we got to the car park.

Again, I considered retrieving that hidden box and telling Jesse what had happened and what it was threatening to do to me. But even the thought of recounting it made me sick to the core.

"But you didn't tell Darcy either," I pointed out, gripping my temples.

"That's true. I guess I wanted to deal with it myself. And it was nice coming to a place where no one else knew. But, how long can you pretend you have a sister when you don't?"

Mum's car came into view. "I'm just there," I said, pointing it out. I thought we'd part ways at that, but Jesse kept walking with me so I kept the conversation going. "Will you tell Darcy? About Minty?"

"Yeah, eventually." And yet he couldn't bring himself to tell Flo. My guess was that he cared more about her reaction than any other and didn't want to be there to see it.

Mum's head appeared above her car. *Why* was she getting out? To meet Jesse?

I felt my nerves spring into action as my brain freeze eased away. I picked up my pace. "Thanks for the slurpee!" I said quickly. But Jesse didn't leave, not even as Mum stormed toward me and I practically melted into the ground.

"I would say you're welcome," he began, "but you got cola so I can't validate that. Paying for it was hard enough."

As Mum approached, rage became plain in every crevice of her face. "Where the *hell* have you *been?*"

For some reason I found myself clutching my slurpee straw between my teeth instead of answering her.

"Uh, sorry—it was my fault," Jesse piped up behind me.

That broke me from my daze enough that I spun to him and hissed, "I'll see you later."

Jesse hesitated a moment, but then finally retreated to his car, raising two fingers in a cautious wave as he went.

Mum's arms were crossed when I turned back. The look on her face coiled my stomach into a knot. "You weren't answering your phone. Why didn't you answer? I was *this* close to calling the police." There was an underlying tremor to her voice that had me forgiving her instantly for making a scene in front of Jesse.

"We got slurpees, Mum. I thought there'd be enough time." I pulled out my phone. Six missed calls. A series of capitalized texts.

Mum: *Where are you?*

Mum: *Dotty???*

Mum: *Are you still inside?*

Mum: *The restaurant lights are off … WHERE ARE YOU?*

Mum: *Your manager says you already left???*

Mum: *DOTTY?????*

I looked up and saw the hardness in her eyes coated with static tears. And I ran over and hugged her.

All Mum's sharp edges folded around me. We stood there together for what felt like an age while she pressed my face into her collarbone so hard that it hurt, as if she thought I might disappear if she let go. I wondered the same thing.

18

RAY

I caught Jesse at the stand tapping an order into the screen. He was a good kid–this was his third year at Corner. I knew I could trust him, even with someone this precious. "When you finish tonight, could you walk out with Dotty?"

"Uh, sure." Jesse gave me an inquiring look, but I just answered it with a nod.

"Thanks kid. Also–contain that mop." I gestured to his hair, which was coming loose around his face.

"Yes boss."

Jude was in the office with his feet up on the desk. He was wearing the checkered shirt that brought out the blue in his eyes and pulled at his arms. "What have I told you?" I said, putting on my gruffest voice, which had Jude rapidly drawing his feet away. "We *must* invest in a TV here."

He offered a rueful smile and rolled his chair toward me. "Plasma screen?"

"Across the entire wall," I said.

Jude smiled and reached out, coiling his hand around my knee. I stepped back fast, then cast a glance around to make sure the kids were still out front.

"Time and place," I hissed. Jude rolled his eyes and his chair back to the computer screen.

"Might I ask if the time will ever be during daylight hours, and if the place will ever be somewhere that isn't my house?" This wasn't the first time he'd said something to this effect, but my answer was still the same.

"Yes, just—not yet."

Was there a simple way to tell your son that despite his obvious conception, you were now attracted to men? And that you were, in fact, in a relationship with one? Who worked for you? Who was fifteen years younger?

"Ray …" Jude lay a hand out flat on the desk. I wished we were somewhere else so I could reach over and take it. "If there's one thing I've learnt in life, it's that if you're waiting for the time to suit you and the place to be right, you'll be waiting forever."

"I know." I slipped my hands into my pockets and squeezed them into tight fists. "I just need a *little* more time."

"It will never be easy."

He was right, but he could never fully understand. There was no kid for him to factor into this equation. No family to consider. His parents knew who he was and celebrated it openly. We'd both experienced different battles, and telling Peter was mine to face alone.

"I'm going to head home," I said. "But, please make sure that when Dotty leaves, Jesse goes with her."

"We need to tell the dubs about the attack," Jude replied, more curtly than was warranted.

"We will."

"All in your time," he drawled.

"Yes, and so it should be," I said, unable to stop the snowball from tumbling out of my control. Building into something too big. "This is my life and my business to run. You manage the restaurant, not me."

Jude was often inscrutable, but this time the hurt was plain on his face.

"I'm sorry." I squeezed my temples with two fingers, massaging the anger away. "I'm just … emotional."

"Clearly," huffed Jude. "Just go home. I'll call you later."

I managed to smile at him, and he managed to muster a thin one of his own.

Jesse was taking meals from the kitchen window. "See you soon," I said. "Remember to walk her out." He nodded and offered a polite nod.

There was an air of respect about him, that Jesse Melrose. His edges were rough, with that wild hair and the piercings I'd told him more than once to take out before clocking in—but he was fiercely loyal.

I decided to wait outside for Dotty. She was due to start in a few minutes.

Soon enough Kat's car pulled up and my sister waved from the driver's window. I watched Dotty clamber out and make her way across to me, but my thoughts were on Kat. Dotty had the same narrow frame as her Mum and even a similar, edgy gait.

Telling Peter would be tough. Telling Kat would be another sort of tough. Our family had been relatively conservative growing up, which is probably why it took me so long to realise what I really wanted. Dad got me into footy, drove me to games every week. He encouraged me to pick up drums too. I loved the sport and the music, and that's likely why coming out seemed such an impossibility. I was doing all the blokey things and enjoying them, so what was the problem?

I'd even married young—to Rhea. We'd been in love, in our own way, but it was short-lived. Ironically, no fault of mine.

Maybe she took off because she could sense something wasn't sitting right between us. But even if that *had* been the case, what she did was unforgivable. Leaving me with Peter—a toddler. No indication of where she went.

I often joked with Jude that Rhea was what turned me off women. It wasn't that simple, but you might say that she helped to reroute me.

When Dotty got to the stairs, I recognised the stiffness in her expression and posture. It was Kat all over. My sister was loud and outspoken, but her wariness was just as overt. She couldn't seem to hide her opinion. That was what troubled me most.

I hadn't seen Darcy since the night of the attack. But I thought of him. A lot. And I let myself, because apart from the fact that he was entirely unattainable, he was preferable to the other thoughts that plagued me at night.

So I remembered the way he looked at me in the car. That adorable frown, etched from genuine concern and determined insistence. His hand resting on my knee as he asked me to tell him what had happened. How he'd almost strangled me with the bandage.

And then back further to our conversation near the bins. I imagined him crossing the space between us and gathering me in his arms. I painted every detail of that false moment as sleep took me, because somehow Darcy could redefine the darkness.

———•———

Darcy: *Hey, just checking in. How you going?*

I was at the dinner table with Mum and Dad when the text came through. Darcy had asked for my number before we parted ways the night of the mugging, but I hadn't thought he'd actually use it. We were rostered on to work together that Saturday. It was a Thursday. He could've waited, but he hadn't. He'd texted.

I read it over as I brushed my teeth, then again after I climbed into bed. The construction of a worthy response took longer than I care to admit.

Me: *Doing okay. They say I was lucky he wasn't stronger, otherwise the bandage could've done some serious damage.*

I wasn't convinced it was funny outside of my head, or that he'd understand, but I sent it anyway and gritted my teeth until my phone buzzed again.

Darcy: *Haha. Maybe this dude needs to spend less time playing soccer and more time lifting weights.*

For the last few nights I'd forced Darcy to the forefront of my mind for the sole purpose of overriding all else. But he was really here this time. I could say anything I wanted and he would see it.

Me: *Are you really deciding how to better prepare for my strangulation?*

His response came faster this time.

Darcy: *I think I am? Not sure how that happened. Sorry. Anyway how you really feeling?*

I stared at the message for a long time, trying to decide how honest to be. Maybe it was due to the streets and screens between us, but I decided to tell him the truth.

Me: *Trying not to think about it - much harder at night.*

Darcy: *It's okay to think about it.*

I didn't know how to tell him that it wasn't, because I was scared. Scared of glimpsing the cut under my jaw, scared of the shadows in my room, scared of letting myself remember and trapping myself in the dark with that faceless figure.

Kramer leapt up onto my bed out of nowhere like my own personal, fluffy guardian angel with a sixth sense for when I needed moral support.

Me: *You still working Saturday?*

Darcy: *Yah. Are you?*

Me: *Yep.*

I let the message hang for a while, and when he didn't respond in five minutes, I sent another.

Me: *Thanks for checking in.*

Darcy: *Of course.*

I set my phone down, thinking that was the end. But a minute later it lit up again.

Darcy: *I'm ordering you a can of pepper spray btw.*

20

"I think you need a hobby, Dorothy."

I gave Mum a withering look. She was standing in the doorway to the living room, arms crossed with this pensive expression, like she'd only just thought of this. But I knew it had been a long time coming.

Since Cameron left, Mum seemed to think I didn't have much left in my life, which only made me feel worse, because I thought it too. And the attack—that had sent her worry into overdrive.

But it was okay, because apparently I could be fixed by taking up knitting or squash or something. This was probably why I didn't have a hobby—since the only hobbies that came to mind when considering hobbies were knitting and squash.

"I think it would be good for you. Take your mind off things." Her voice was light enough but her shoulders were just about at her ears. "Your Dad found this place that hosts indoor sports just down the road. You've probably seen it, near the Woolies?"

I tried not to move, not to breathe. If I compelled my body to turn completely unresponsive, she might stop there.

"Dotty?" She perched on the couch arm beside me and I locked my phone. I'd been googling pepper spray–which Mum didn't need to see–to check if it was really a thing you could buy. General consensus was no. It was illegal to carry in Australia. You could be fined for carrying a knife, too. Any sort of knife. So … if someone came at you wielding one, you basically had your keys to scratch back and your legs to get away. Great.

"The last time I made a suggestion like this you ended up thanking me for it," Mum said.

"Really?" I finally looked up at her. "I thought I ended up getting mugged in a car park." It was a low blow and I'm not really sure where it came from, but I instantly wanted to stuff it back in my mouth because Mum looked like she'd been slapped.

I backpedalled fast. "I'm sorry, that was silly. Sorry Mum. You're right, Corner was good for me."

"It's all right," she said sharply. "I just thought you might enjoy to fill your time with something apart from work over the summer."

"I know. I'll give it a think." I said it mostly to thwart the guilt still hanging over me, but she appeared somewhat appeased.

When I went into work on Saturday, Darcy was already in the back office with Jude.

"It's the big black container," Jude was saying. "Seriously, it's the best out and it will last you a *long* time. But you have to get vanilla."

Darcy glanced across at me and his face cracked into a wry smile that seemed to make my heart leap into my throat. He pointed at Jude, who was swivelling back and forth in his chair. "Protein powder talk," Darcy said. "What brand do you recommend Dot?"

I chewed on my lip and pretended to consider. "The powdery one, I'd suggest. Definitely powdery."

Darcy nodded along. "Oh, nice. I'll check it out."

We clocked in and crossed with Reese, who had been rostered on a double–lunch as a dub and dinner as a bartender. He couldn't look more comfortable behind the bar, and it seemed everyone that came to the stools there entered into his bubble of ease, judging by the near-constant, hearty laughter from the back.

Emma had taken Flo's shift on the machine again. I wondered if Flo was okay. She normally worked Saturday's. Did she still think something was going on between me and Jesse? Is that why she wasn't here?

It seemed a trivial train of thought in the light of those that were much heavier. But even they were eased by Darcy's presence. We busied ourselves around tables and food and drinks—but I was hyper alert to wherever he went. Our synchronized visits to the kitchen were a chance for rapid conversation, and at the stand we got to speak for a little longer. Nothing about the mugging, mostly just mockery of our rudest customers and subtle digs at one another.

Halfway through the night Darcy asked me for a fun fact about myself. It threw me off, as those questions often did, like I was suddenly a desolate nothingness without a single point of interest.

I told him I'd get back to him, and we diverged to our tables. When we reconvened, Darcy pouring waters and me retrieving extra napkins for a table of lively toddlers, I said, "I like to collect things. Business cards mostly, but when I go somewhere I want to remember, I take something away."

I'd told Jesse as much. About the business cards at least.

"So you steal." Darcy said it seriously, but then grinned at me when I turned to him. It was a playful look that coiled my stomach into a knot.

"Essentially." I took the napkins to the toddlers who had proceeded to smear potato mash across the table, mostly ignored by their oblivious, wine-drinking parents.

Darcy was scraping plates free of food scraps when I came into the kitchen with a tower of dirty glasses. "Your turn." I knocked his elbow with mine. It was an affectionate gesture that I probably should've resisted, but I felt energetic and bold tonight. Being around Darcy helped me forget everything else.

He hesitated, and I wondered for a moment if he'd forgotten the game. Then he said, "I hate tomato. Like, absolutely despise it. I don't know if it's the texture or what, but I can't do it. I just can't."

I suppressed a laugh as Emma piped up. "Darc, honestly, you're so difficult."

He shrugged at her and then crinkled his nose at me before we parted again.

Throughout the rest of the shift I learned that Darcy played bass guitar, studied Business like me—only one year ahead and at Monash instead of Swinburne, that he dyed his hair blue in year 10, and he loved going for long drives.

He learned that I wished I had a sibling, that most of my friends from high school didn't speak to me anymore because I neglected them for a guy, a guy who broke things off to study in America, and that I too could live without tomato.

This series of admissions brought Darcy to an equally significant one. "I've been dating Nina since high school," he said at the stand, while he reached for knives and forks. "But I think we're … growing apart, in a way. Like, we've both changed a lot since then."

I considered sharing that my Dad had a high school sweetheart before my Mum swooped in, and look at them now. But I wouldn't want him to think I was damning the relationship. Although, statistically speaking, a lot of high school relationships didn't last. Most of my friends had broken up with guys they'd dated in school a few years out.

In my opinion, it was because life was a sequence of bubbles. Every bubble held a certain collection of people, and when you were stuck for so long in the high school bubble, you came to feel like it was all there was. And then when you ventured outside of it, you saw more and started to wonder if you were intended to take what you found in the first bubble into the next, or the one after, and so on.

Of course I said none of this to Darcy.

The last customer left at half past ten, and we began close. Chairs tilted. Tables wiped. Darcy's guitar-ridden music blaring. I would text Mum soon to let her know we were finishing up.

I tied the bin bag and headed for the back alley. It was only as I stepped into the night that I started to feel the weight bearing down again. Darcy had kept it from smothering me for most of the night, but it was returning with a vengeance and my stroll turned into a frantic dash toward the bin.

I chucked the bag over its edge. It hit the side and fell to the ground. I didn't stop to pick it up. I raced back into the restaurant, breathing hard and fast.

Darcy caught me by the shoulders. "Hey, you all good?"

"Yeah," I lied.

He dropped his hands and glanced outside. "Your car isn't here."

"Mum's picking me up."

"Oh." A pause. "I can drop you?"

If my heart wasn't racing before, it sure was now. "You don't have to do that."

"Nah, nah, it's cool. Where do you live?"

"Trace Street."

"Oh yeah, I know it. It isn't far from me."

I thanked him and ran into the back office to text Mum.

Got a ride home. Don't worry, all safe. See you later x

And soon enough I was walking out of Corner and climbing into Darcy's silver Mazda.

He grabbed the papers at my feet before I sat, spreading them across the back seat. "Sorry," he said. "Just all my uni crap."

"It's okay."

There was a pause in conversation as he fussed over the papers. I felt so uncomfortable I almost told him not to bother with the drive–that I'd text Mum and she would come to get me right away.

We'd been alone together in a car before. But there were bigger things than awkward small talk to worry about that night.

Just as I opened my mouth to fabricate an excuse like *Mum just texted me saying she already left home*, Darcy spun back to the front and stared at me with this expectant glint in his eye. It took me a moment to look lower and realise he was holding something out.

I took it from his palm, frowning as I read the label. "Pepper?"

"Turns out pepper spray is illegal to carry in Australia, did you know that? Yeah." I was already laughing, but Darcy kept on. "This was the closest thing I could find." The car rumbled to life, setting the radio blasting and me jumping. He turned it right down as we pulled out of the car park. "Might not have the same effect, but we have to take what we can get."

"Did you seriously buy me pepper? As a mode of defense?"

"Uh-huh." He nodded and the corner of his mouth twitched.

It was a small, glass cylinder—the sort of pepper you grind. A shaker would have been better, really. Grinding could waste valuable seconds. I told Darcy as much as we stopped at the first set of lights.

He answered as if taking what I said very seriously. "You could be right. But maybe it will have the opposite effect. Because I mean how confused would you be if you went to mug someone and they started grinding pepper on you? It would give you pause for thought, surely."

He was speaking so casually about what I'd been fighting hard to forget, that I was left stumped. All I could do was stare.

"Well, thanks," I said. "This is the weirdest, sweetest thing anyone's ever done for me." Maybe that was an exaggeration, maybe it wasn't. But I wanted to say it anyway.

"Use it wisely," he said. "But seriously, I hope you're doing okay. You heard anything more from the police?"

"No." I wished people would stop asking me that. I set the pepper grinder on my lap and turned to the window.

"Do you want to talk about it?"

"I'm not sure." I realised shortly after saying it that I wasn't being very helpful at all, and if anyone had said the same thing to me I'd be left extremely confused as to where to take the conversation. I felt guilty for putting Darcy in that position, but really didn't know what else to add.

"You mentioned it was harder at night," he said, seemingly unperturbed. "Do you dream about it?"

My face felt hot, like a giant spotlight was suddenly illuminating the fact that yes, I did dream about that night, and yes, I did use Darcy to allevi-ate the nightmares.

"Most nights," I admitted, before clearing my throat and giving myself permission to be a little more honest. "It's like … well, I've always been sort of jumpy, I guess. And now it's as if I'm constantly teetering on the edge of panic."

"Mmm." I let myself look across at Darcy as he made a series of thinking noises. Streetlights slunk across his dark blonde hair, which was just long enough at the top to tuck behind his ears. "That must be exhausting." It wasn't a lengthy response, but it was perfectly accurate. "How did your parents react?"

"I think it shook them up a bit," I said, "consider-ing Mum is insisting on picking me up from every-where for the rest of my life."

Darcy snorted a laugh. "I don't really blame her."

"You know my Dad still calls you Liam Neeson," I told him.

"No shit." He looked genuinely chuffed. "That's so funny."

Another silence, this time longer. It didn't feel so awkward anymore, though. At last Darcy asked me if I'd spoken to anyone else about the attack. *Flo? Jesse?* I told him truthfully that I hadn't, and then wondered if he felt similarly to how I did when Jesse confided in me about his sister–that we might share a connection now, stronger than before.

I was beginning to see that this is what honesty did, what sharing with the right person could do. It was binding. It drew a thread from your heart to theirs and yanked you closer together, whether you wanted it to or not.

And that, I realised, was probably why I had felt so alone over the past year and a half. There were no connecting threads—just me, tangled in my own.

———•———

Outside my house, I thanked Darcy for the pepper and the ride and swung my bag over a shoulder. He said my name as I went to shut the car door. I had to reach and open it again.

"Remember when we were talking about the stars and how they're so much brighter out in the country?"

"Yeah?"

"Just—don't forget them. No matter how dark it looks up there."

21

I set Darcy's pepper between a shell I collected from Sorrento's back beach last year and the Smirnoff lid from Reese's party. Nearing the shelf's left edge was a faded teddy bear key ring from Cameron I forgot to throw out. That photo of him and Miss Short Dress on Facebook came to mind, so I grabbed the bear and tossed it to the floor to bin later, dragging the pepper forward.

I got into my favourite pyjamas, blue with white polka dots, and lay on my bed to think over what Darcy had said.

Don't forget them. No matter how dark it looks up there.

He seemed a little embarrassed after having voiced the sentiment, but not as embarrassed as I was in trying and failing to articulate an adequate response.

Kramer appeared then, with Cameron's key ring caught between his teeth. He didn't often chew things to pieces, just pawed at them or hoarded them. So I decided to let him keep it. If he did happen to tear it to shreds–all the better.

I switched my lamp off and forced a steadying breath. A familiar, tight feeling pressed in around me, like it had been waiting for an opportunity.

No matter how dark it looks …

Stars. Billions of stars. I closed my eyes and imagined the ceiling opening up to reveal each one glistening above. I cast myself up, up, up to meet them. But I made myself bigger, so that when I got there, I could reach out and hold them in my hands.

Slowly, they began blinking out. Disappearing into nothing. The dark grew larger and wrapped an iron grip around my neck. It pulled. Strangled. I was fading, just like the stars. None of us were any match for the blackness.

I gasped into waking. Immediate terror shrouded any sense of calm as I flicked on the light and snapped my attention to every corner of the room. It was much the same as it had been before I fell asleep.

You're safe. You're alone.

I repeated the words over and over until another nightmare took me, as if intent on proving me wrong.

———◆———

The next night Mum, Dad and I went to Uncle Ray's for dinner. We alternated houses every second week.

It was cool for a summer's night, so I rugged up in my softest woolly jumper. The sky was bright enough for my heart to rest easy as we made our way to the car. Halfway there, my phone buzzed.

Flo: *Hey, want to get milkshakes before work Tuesday?*

I'd almost expected it to be from Darcy, but this was good too. My fears had consumed so much of my mental energy that I'd neglected to arrange a proper meet up with Flo. I needed to tell her about Jesse and his sister, and how it might have affected his decisions back when they'd been an *almost*. I also needed to clarify that nothing had happened between us at Reese's. And maybe I wanted to talk about Darcy too.

Me: *Would love to. Same place we had Melbourne's best ice cream?*

Flo: *Where else?*

"Who are you smiling at?" Mum asked from the front seat.

I looked up from my phone, wiping the smile away because I didn't want her to get too excited I had friends now and say something like *didn't I tell you Corner would be good for you?* "No one."

"Is it that boy who dropped you home last night?"

"No, Mum." I came down quickly to thwart the hope in her voice. She must've been at the window when Darcy pulled up. Fantastic. I hoped to God he hadn't seen her.

I remembered Flo telling me about the guy she once snuck through her window. That would never fly in my house. Not because my parents were uber-strict, but because they would hijack any boy coming to visit me and end up chatting to him themselves all night. Mum and Dad, though vastly different as the salted caramel combo they were, could talk any ear off.

"Who's this?" Dad piped up, as if Mum hadn't told him already. She would have. "Liam Neeson?"

"*Dad*." How did he always *know*? I forced my voice into a perfectly balanced mix of calm and casual. "He has a girlfriend."

"Ah, the age old–*he has a girlfriend*," drawled Dad, casting a wry smile Mum's way. "Sound familiar, dear?"

Her lips turned tight, but I could see she was holding back a return smile. When they met, Dad had a girlfriend already. I'd heard the story a million times before. Apparently it was a scandal at the time, for all involved.

"Don't twist our daughter's moral compass, Jim."

Dad held his hands up in earnest, momentarily driving with his knees. This earned him a less amused glare from Mum.

I didn't want to discuss Darcy, so I turned to the window and thought about him instead.

———◆———

Peter answered the door still in his work suit, which was pale-grey and tailored to a tee. He hugged Mum and shook Dad's hand, and then stopped at me, giving me this exasperated look.

He shook his head and said, "What are you doing, going around getting robbed for?" I knew he was joking, but that didn't stop me from wanting to whack him over the head. "Come here, you peanut." He gave me an awkward one-armed hug and kept his arm around my neck as we went inside.

He and Uncle Ray lived in a modern apartment in Richmond and ordered UberEats for almost every meal, including tonight's. The décor vaguely followed a black and white theme, and the kitchen table was always half-covered in papers, pushed to the end to make room for dinner.

Uncle Ray travelled to Sydney and Queensland a fair bit, to check on the Corner restaurants up there. That was probably why their apartment was in a constant state of disarray. It wasn't like Peter would clean up.

"Hope you're hungry," Uncle Ray said, setting two stacks of plastic tubs on the table. "They made a mistake with the order so we ended up with double. That side is spicy as hell, Jim, so steer clear."

We made it through half the dinner before Peter decided to bring up the mugging.

"So tell me how it happened," he said to me, without warning. "Dad tried to explain, but I want a play-by-play from the horse's mouth."

I stuffed that horse's mouth with noodles to buy me some time, just as Mum swooped in.

"Peter, you just won't believe it. *I* still can't believe it." She started going on about how I'd looked coming home that night, *pale and completely unresponsive*, apparently.

She was onto our trip to the police station when I forced myself to tune out. A coldness settled over me, freezing out the conversation and the memories it threatened to bring back.

Pounding heart. Rough voice. Unfamiliar. Close. Thick air. A blade–sharp. Cutting.

It was only when I drew a shuddering breath that my senses returned. All four faces were on me. Dad's hand was laid over Mum's, as though he was midway through an unspoken warning.

"You all right, girl?" Uncle Ray asked. I appreciated the way he said it–in his standard, no-nonsense manner. Like if I said *yes* he would actually believe it.

Blood rushed into my cheeks and I forced my face to relax, realising then that I'd bitten into my lip so hard there was blood there too. I could taste it.

"Yeah," I said. "I'm fine."

My hand was trembling as I picked up the fork again. I wound noodles around it and kept on eating while Mum busied herself with a hurried change of subject.

22

Mint and banana–I hadn't tried it before, but it made so much sense. Flo was adamant it would be the best milkshake I'd ever had. I told her it was, even though nothing could trump a Macca's chocolate thickshake.

We headed down towards Marley Park, which wasn't far from the ice cream shop. So far our conversation had only touched the very surface of our respective lives–work rosters, Flo's painting, my uni semester finishing. I didn't know how to bring up Jesse, or the night of Reese's party.

As we approached the park, conversation petered out. But when we both gravitated toward the same seesaw as last time, claiming opposite sides, I felt a dormant connection spring to life again. Maybe seeing the literal line between us was reminder enough. Or maybe the silence was starting to drag, and I knew that if I didn't say something now I never would.

"Hey, sorry I didn't get to speak to you at Reese's party the other week."

"Oh." Flo raised her brows, as if she were genuinely taken aback. "No, no. No dramas." Well, that couldn't be further from the truth.

"Actually I was talking to Jesse," I said, careful to channel my best attempt at nonchalance. "He told me something you might want to know."

That arrested her attention completely, her bright-blue eyes wide on me as she sucked on her straw.

I ploughed on. "Did you know he had a sister?"

"Minty," she said, swallowing. "He talks about her some—wait … had?"

I sighed, hoping I hadn't misinterpreted Jesse's request for me to pass this on. "She died last year. From cancer."

Flo stared at me, frozen.

"I think it wasn't long after that you two … yeah. And he was dealing with a lot at the time. He didn't want to tell people back then. But now, I think now is different."

"Oh no." Flo's lips barely parted as she spoke, like they were frozen too. "He never let on. Never said a thing. Why wouldn't he tell me? Any of us? We could've … done something."

I shrugged. People were different, which meant no one person really knew what any other person needed, or when they needed it.

When I was eleven, Grandma was dying in hospital while Mum, Dad, Uncle Ray, Peter and I sat around her bed. I remembered Uncle Ray was talking the whole time, not even about Grandma but about the weather and about Corner. Mum had practically exploded. Like, really shouted at him. He left the room at that point and missed the moment Grandma went. He didn't need silence. What he needed was to talk, as if she was sitting in her favourite armchair listening too.

"I guess he's telling you now," I said to Flo.

She frowned. "But he told *you,* not me."

"He wanted me to tell you."

"Really? He said that?"

"Mhm."

We bobbed up and down a few times, going back to our milkshakes. The sun had melted mine so that the paper cup was sweating tracks around my fingers.

"Poor Jesse," Flo muttered. "His poor *family.* Should I say anything?"

"I'm not sure," I admitted. "I don't know if he wanted you to say anything, so much as just … know."

A woman holding a young boy came into view. She set him on the grass and he charged at the swings, not unlike Emma had done, and we watched him for a while.

"I wish I'd known sooner," Flo said, chewing on her straw. There was a sincere despair in her voice that made me like her all the more. Then her gaze fell back on me and she touched her neck. "What happened there?"

"Uh …" I brought my fingers over the long scab. "Just, scissors." Good one.

It wasn't the time to bring up the attack, but I felt like I could if I wanted to. I felt like I could tell Flo anything—so long as we stayed on the seesaw sipping on our milkshakes.

23

When Saturday came around, the edge of my panic felt a little further off than it had before. I was excited to see Darcy again. I couldn't help it and I wouldn't if I could.

Flo was working in the kitchen. Since our milk-shake date, things were easier with her. The air was mostly clear—clear enough that she'd invited me over to her house after work. I'd managed to convince Mum to let me drive to Corner, so that I could go straight there.

Things were looking up, aside from the customer I served who insisted their steak was over-cooked three times and had me take it back to the kitchen over and over, refusing to pay in the end.

I'd dealt with angry customers before—well, stood there and stared at them as they yelled at me. The last time it had happened, Emma saved the day. But now I was on my own, and somehow able to string more than a sentence together.

"I'm sorry it wasn't to your satisfaction," I told the man, who was all grey hair and a beetroot-pink face.

"I can get my manager, if you'd like to speak with him?" Yes, he would.

I sighed on my way to the back office. Jude was wearing a short-sleeved shirt that cut sharply into his biceps, leaning intently into the computer screen as he swayed in time to the music. I explained the situation quickly, and he was off his chair before I even finished.

"Not your fault, darling," he said on his way out. "Some people are just looking for a reason to be unhappy."

For a moment I just stood in the doorway to the back office, gazing out at the restaurant. At Darcy, a plate in each hand and one in the crook of his elbow as he moved off from the kitchen to deliver them.

Jude was right. Some people fabricated their own unhappiness. I wondered then if that's what I was doing with Darcy. Because there was no *me and him*, not really. He had someone already. So what was I doing, investing so much time and energy into it all?

Heaviness settled over my shoulders and I had to physically drag myself out from hiding. Jude tapped my shoulder on his way back to the office. "I refunded the meal—he was an arsehole, don't worry."

I moved back to the stand and looked over my tables. In taking only a couple of minutes' time to breathe, I was behind. Drinks needed delivering, orders taken, and an elderly lady near the door had dropped an arancini ball and was trying to pick it up, but it was falling apart, crumbs scattering everywhere.

With a shaky breath, I brushed hair out of my face and dived into the melee.

———•———

Flo finished the kitchen close before me and Darcy. Even though she'd already clocked out, she took a washer from the stand and helped me wipe down the last few tables. Darcy was taking the bins out when the door to Corner swung open.

I didn't recognise her right away. She was taller than I remembered, wearing black skinny jeans, a puffy jacket and this removed, searching look.

"Hey Nina," Flo said, throwing her rag back to the stand bench.

I was going to say hello too, but she hardly looked our way. "Hey–do you know where Darcy is?"

"Bin duty," Flo answered. "He'll be back soon."

I risked a glance up at Nina, seeing her mouth turn down irritably at the side. From what little I'd seen of her, she seemed the complete opposite of Darcy. He was all smiles and warmth, but she was about as emotive as a plank of wood. Both Jesse and Flo could see that he deserved more. Why couldn't he?

I straightened away from the table and noticed Nina's eyes on me. "You're Dot, right?" she asked, knocking the breath from my lungs and words from my head so all I could do was nod. "Oh God." She frowned, the way you might frown at a dog with three legs. "Darcy told me everything. Did they end up catching the guy?"

I opened my mouth to respond and out came my hugely unhelpful, lifelong accomplice–silence.

"What guy?" Flo said behind me.

"It's–it's nothing." Hurt burned through me as Darcy reappeared to steal Nina's attention.

"Hey." He squeezed her shoulder on his way to the office. "I'll just grab my bag."

We were left again in a tense quiet, which grew to an exceptional level of awkward as Darcy's music was switched off too.

"Dot?" Flo spoke my name quietly, as if trying to evade Nina's awareness. Nina herself was now leaning against a table, scrolling on her phone. Probably to escape the awkward turn in the conversation.

I didn't care what Nina thought of me though. I cared that Darcy had told her about the attack when he'd promised not to share it with a single soul. I cared that our only mutual understanding had been stolen away because he'd used it to connect with someone else, like what happened didn't matter.

I cared that the girl I'd tried to ignore was standing here in front of me, waiting for the boy I liked too much to finish work so they could go home together.

I cared. I cared. I cared too much. And just like that—the band-aid came away, and I saw that the wound hadn't healed. Not even a little bit.

24

Flo held onto me fiercely while I cried and sniffled into her shoulder. We were standing in the bathroom at Corner. Nina and Darcy had left moments ago—and it was only then that I couldn't hold myself together any longer. I had unravelled, right into Flo's arms.

When I turned my head I saw us framed in the mirror. I was hunched into her and her back was arched to hold me. I looked small and weak, like everything I despised about myself. And I started to feel unbearably silly. Much bigger things happened to people in this world, so why was I crumbling? And why now?

"I'm sorry," I mumbled. "This is stupid."

"No." She sighed. "You bottled up something really, really scary. You could've told me, you know. Why do people think it's better to deal with these things alone?"

I knew who she meant. I pulled away from her, wiping at my eyes. "I didn't want to admit how much I still … felt it."

Flo folded her arms and angled her head. "There's no shame in that." She hesitated, her eyes flickering lower. "That cut—is it from …"

I muttered a yes. Flo sighed again and drew me in, briefly this time. "Let's go back to mine," she said. "Dad brought home these cookies yesterday you gotta try. And Jude's probably about to lock us in."

As we walked out to my car, I thought of Darcy again. How senseless I'd been to assume we were somehow intimately linked by what happened that night. Nina probably knew about the pepper joke too. For some reason, I found myself wondering whether she'd come up with it herself, even though I knew that was unlikely.

"Want me to drive?" Flo offered.

"No, it's okay." I was eager to leave the sobbing, ineffectual child behind in the Corner bathroom.

We were quiet most of the way to Flo's. When we got there she insisted I stay the night, so I called Mum to let her know. Judging by the caution in her voice, she must have suspected I was with a boy. Maybe even the boy she'd seen drop me home— Liam Neeson. *The one with the girlfriend*. To allevi- ate any such suspicions, I told her a little about Flo and where she lived and that seemed to satisfy her enough.

Flo's Dad helped us pump a mattress on her bedroom floor, amidst the mess of paints and paper. She even loaned me a pair of purple, silk pyjamas—much more dignified than any I owned—and went out in search of cookies and milk while I changed.

Unsurprisingly, the pyjama sleeves fell well past my wrists and the pants slid under my heels due to Flo's long, slender frame. It felt nice to wear clothes that weren't mine though. My thoughts were my own—there was nothing I could do about that. But the outside could be changed. And I wanted to change what I could.

Flo returned with a plate of cookies and two glasses. I set up on the floor mattress despite her protests—as if I'd let her give up her bed for me—and she sat cross-legged on her bed.

I gazed around at the paintings, left half in shadow since the light of Flo's bedside lamp was mottled by strings of beads hanging down around the globe. The paintings were mostly the same, but there were a couple of new additions. One of clouds streaking through a pink sky. Another a face—her Dad's, if I had to guess—with flowers over his eyes.

It was as I looked at the paintings and munched on the cookies that I decided to confide in Flo. She was reserved, private in how she spoke and what she said or didn't say. But simply bringing me into her creative haven was an act of honesty. And I wanted to reciprocate.

"Can I tell you something silly?"

Flo snorted and a cookie crumb shot out of her mouth. She tapped her lips as if to scold them for letting it go. I couldn't help but laugh, mostly because it was surprising from someone so typically composed. "Silly is your favourite word," she said, still tapping her mouth. "But nothing you've ever said has sounded silly."

"Well, this might be a first then." I swished the milk around in my glass, creating a small whirlpool that I could watch while I spoke. "You know how I said Darcy found me that night?"

"Uh-huh."

"Well, we started talking more, after everything. And I came to …" I hesitated, searching for the right way to voice the confession. "I came to really like him."

I expected that I might need to elaborate. But I didn't have to, because Flo had paused mid-chew, silent, her big blue eyes even bigger.

"Oh, wow." She pressed a finger to her lips–her nails were painted sky blue. "You would make the cutest couple."

I wasn't sure if it was what I needed to hear, but I let myself grin anyway. "I've been thinking about him a lot, and I know he has Nina and that's why it's silly. But it's easier to think about him than it is to think about the rest of that night."

Flo nodded slowly, considering. She didn't appear to think it was silly at all, unless she was just really good at hiding it. I dismissed the thought and battled on, keeping my eyes on Flo's painting of the sky.

"Then tonight I realised he'd told Nina about it, and she became real, and all of my stupid fantasies fell away to uncover something … painful."

I heard Flo shift and risked a glance her way. She was on her back, facing the ceiling. "It sounds to me like there are two layers to this." I found myself smiling. It had been a long time since I'd had a self-analytical conversation with a friend. A long time since I'd had a friend at all. "One—you like Darcy, and you're sad that he's unattainable. And two—you were using him to distract yourself from the trauma of that night. So when Nina shows up, all, *oh my gawd, have they caught the guy*?—it's a dagger to the heart—sorry, bad analogy … it made you realise your feelings for Darcy, I mean, *and* how you feel about the attack."

It's a conclusion I would have drawn myself, but I liked hearing Flo talk it out. Because it was outside of me. My mind often felt like a prison, a single cell in the middle of nowhere. But someone else had found it now, and could at least speak to me through the bars.

We talked well past midnight. I told her all about Darcy—the texts, the pepper, our conversations at Corner. The floodgates had opened, and I couldn't stop the outpour.

Although, it seemed the more I said, the more she said too. One admission in exchange for another—an unspoken trade deal.

Flo had fallen for Jesse the moment they met. He was sharp and cheeky where she was sensible, and bold with his art where she hid hers. She told me how much she admired him for his photography alone, and that's when I recalled something he'd said to me at Reese's.

"He found your paintings online," I told her. "A portfolio of your work or something."

Flo gasped and twisted to face me. "Are you serious?"

"Yep."

"He never said." Her tone had changed. She sounded almost nervous.

"He never said a lot of things, it seems."

Flo sunk back onto her bed, pulling the sheets up to her chin. "So he was looking. He must've Google searched." She hesitated. "Have you done one on Darc?"

I laughed. "No, actually."

In a few short moments Flo had her laptop out in front of her, and I was perched up beside her while we flicked through Darcy's ancient soccer results, an article from his school newsletter—he got 89.8 in his final exams—and a few stray photos of him on Google images. One in particular had me dissolving into a fit of laughter. He'd told me about his *blue hair* stage, but seeing it was something else. The photo was taken on a webcam and his expression was stone cold under a stark, blue fringe swept over one eye.

Flo laughed too, like I'd never heard before. Her shoulders shook and this bizarre hiss escaped her, which only made us laugh harder.

"He should bring it back," she suggested, once we'd composed ourselves. "It might repel Nina."

"Hopefully," I said, before I could stop myself.

Flo shut her laptop with a heavy sigh. "I want to ask Jesse about Minty. Or, at least tell him I'm here if he wants to talk."

"Then tell him," I said, inspired by the boldness of all our confessions. I made myself think it over a moment longer. "But wait for the right time. Maybe reach out to him again. The worst that can happen is nothing." It was like listening to a stranger speak. Usually, I was fantastic at imagining *the worst that could happen*.

"Okay, yes. I'll try making an effort with him in general, and then just play it by ear."

Before we went to sleep, I asked Flo to show me more of her work. So, out came the sketchbook. Three sketchbooks, actually. She flipped through them and explained the meaning behind everything. This time she didn't try to hide the pages that were clearly inspired by Jesse. She just sighed and gave me this sad, rueful smile, saying things like, *I know*, and *I just paint what's on my mind*.

Her mind must have been a busy place then, I considered. Like mine. Only hers had a route of escape. Colour and strokes and lines tracing her thoughts.

Maybe that was what I needed. A small window in my cell where I could glimpse the sky and tell the stars and the moon how I was feeling. How I wished I could be free like them.

25

The next day I went on a journal hunt. There was this gift shop in a strip of stores near our place that stocked all these cute, eclectic ornaments and jewellery. I didn't go there often for fear of buying out the whole store.

But today I was moving toward a particular stand I recalled by the door. It was filled with beautiful notebooks–leather-bound, gilded covers, parchment pages or crisp, white paper. Each was different, and that's what I loved.

After half an hour of spinning it in a circle to inspect every row, I came away with a teal, hardback notebook with silver edging. It wasn't as elaborate as the other designs, but special and lovely in a more subtle way.

"Good choice," the lady at the counter said, and I wondered if she would've said the same thing no matter what I chose.

Back home I zoomed past Mum en route to my room. If she saw the journal she'd ask too many questions. This was an experimental exercise. Flo's suggestion.

"Have you written down how you're feeling?" she'd asked me last night. I told her no, but the more I thought about it, the more the idea appealed to me.

I liked to write, but I rarely set aside time for it. Back at school, English had been my favourite subject. Mrs Wilson taught us, this elegant, older teacher with grey hair spun into tight curls. I got the impression she secretly hung her highest hopes on me. Well, it wasn't really a secret—she told me as much. But I'd felt her eyes on me from year ten to year twelve, from the moment she read my first essay.

I'd written about this refugee kid leaving his home country to enter Australia, but when he got here, there was nothing left. Everything had been destroyed. So it turned into this post-apocalyptic spin on immigration. To be honest, I wasn't really sure what point I'd been trying to make, but Mrs Wilson ate it up. She told me it was the most thoughtful, intriguing take on the topic she'd ever read.

But I enjoyed Business too, and it seemed the more sensible choice for a career when it came down to electing uni courses at the end of year twelve.

I never forgot the look Mrs Wilson gave me when I told her about my decision. The resigned sigh and that deep, folded frown, like she'd known exactly the direction I should have taken, and what I'd chosen wasn't it. She just told me to keep writing.

But aside from dry, business essays and reflections, I hadn't followed her advice. Maybe this was a chance to change that.

After rifling through my desk drawer I finally found a pen that wasn't all dried up inside. It wasn't surprising that it took so long to find, really. I typed all my assignments for uni—the last time I put pen to paper was probably during exams.

I curled up in my hand chair and flipped to the first page. Blank. Crisp.

This is pointless.

The thought circled. Lingered. But I managed to dismiss it by scribbling the date in the top right corner.

Then I pressed the pen into the paper until it formed an ugly blotch, and eventually, I broke free of it and wrote.

Dot's Journal

I could start with Dear Diary. Ten years ago I probably would have. But now I've come to realise that 'Diary' is just another word for 'me'. A way to make a little girl writing in her room feel less alone. A way to make it seem like she's sharing a secret with someone who cares. The enigmatic Diary.

But the pages won't respond or have any opinions to share. They'll only reflect what I give them. Allow me the space to untangle everything I'm feeling until it's a line I can run my eyes across. It might be a crooked line, but that's better than the jumble of loose ends I've been dealing with.

So here I am, talking to myself. I do a lot of that. Talking to Flo seemed to help a bit, and I'm hoping this will be the same because it's a similar extraction - making the internal external.

I'll start with a few confessions …

1. I'm terrified of strangers.
2. I'm terrified of what people think of me.
3. I'm terrified of having my heart broken.

When I see it laid out like that, it isn't hard to pick up on the fact that most of what I do or don't do revolves around fear. A fear of attack or judgment or hurt.

I don't get it, because there's so much to be grateful for. I have a family that loves me, a body that runs and jumps and generally does all the right things, and I've started making friends. Real ones, I think.

But the attack has drawn my three fears into a rigid knot. I'm more terrified of strangers than I've ever been before, because look what they have the power to do. I'm scared that if people know about it, they'll feel sorry for me. And I feel so silly for letting a boy override it all, a boy who doesn't like me back.

You know what's even sillier? Now that I've mentioned Darcy, I want to keep writing about him. I want to write about my insignificant crush even in the light of a potentially near-death experience.

Does that make me insane?

Sometimes I wonder what it would be like to exist inside somebody else's head. Would everything feel so overwhelming there? Or would it feel like moving from a war-torn country to a beach in Fiji or something. Would the car park attack cripple someone else in the way it's doing to me?

I think. I think. I think. I think because the voices are loud and insistent and they don't ever stop. Our minds are cages without keys. We can share a little but never the whole lot. We can't let someone else inside. That would be impossible. And so we're all stuck with ourselves. Eternal isolation, or maybe damnation. If we don't like who we are, there lies the problem. And maybe it's mine.

It doesn't help when other people decide you're not worth sticking around for either, because they're only confirming what you already feel.

So what now? The walls of my cage are telling me I can't change and fear is inevitable.

Maybe the only answer is to minimize the triggers. Keep away from strangers, keep away from feelings, keep away from feeling anything. Then the fear might finally leave me alone.

26

I spent five days in my bedroom. I came out for meals, and to feed Kramer, but that was about it. I'd almost filled the entire teal notebook.

Dad worked all day, so he didn't question my hibernation too much. Mum was the real problem, regularly coming by my room to frown at me. But I told her I needed the time to myself–that I'd found a hobby. There wasn't much she could say to that, considering she was the one who suggested I take one up.

Uncle Ray had been totally cool when I texted asking for a break from Corner. I didn't want to go to work. Didn't want to see Darcy or deal with the drama there. I couldn't help but hold onto my bitterness over Nina's questions.

My room was safe and forgiving. So was the journal. It didn't ask questions, it just waited for me to speak, and that was what I needed.

I let the memories seep back, let myself feel the panic and the terror of the car park. Instead of turning away from the shadows, I stared into them and watched them move. I forced myself not to use

Darcy as a distraction from the nightmares, knowing it wouldn't do me any good.

Even when he texted me: *Hey Dot, Ray says you're not coming in this week? You okay?* I didn't respond. It was cold, and maybe a little melodramatic, but necessary.

Flo was my main point of contact with the Corner bunch. I let her know that I was all right but didn't want to come out. Couldn't. I'd tapped into something important and couldn't pry myself free just yet.

I poured myself into words, and there was release in that. When night came and the pen came down, I melded with the shadows and wrapped them around every part of myself. It was an odd comfort, but a comfort all the same.

Another week passed. Mum was getting edgy.

"Dotty, honey..." she said, perching all high-shouldered on my bed. "I'm worried about you."

I hit the space bar on my laptop to pause the film I was watching. Subtitles were difficult to delve back into if you missed even a line of them. "Why's that?"

Mum sighed and said, "It's been almost two weeks, and you haven't left the house once."

"I've been writing."

"Writing what?"

"Just, general stuff," I told her.

"Dorothy." Uh-oh. My full name typically preceded things I'd rather not hear. "Is this the best way to move forward?"

"Yes," I said. "I need …" *to get it out of me. I need to make my slippery thoughts tangible.* She wouldn't get it, so I stopped.

She sighed and said, "You're isolating yourself."

My defenses sprang up between us, hard as stone. "And?"

"It isn't healthy, honey. I thought you were doing well–making friends at Corner. What happened to them?"

They aren't going anywhere, I wanted to say. Only, I wasn't sure it was true. Flo would stick around, it seemed, but the others would probably forget about me in no time unless I showed my face again.

But I couldn't. Stepping out the front door suddenly seemed impossible. The dark in my room I could face. Just. The dark outside was another thing altogether.

"You seemed okay after the attack," Mum said carefully. "You were the one that insisted on working, on getting back into a rhythm–"

"I don't know what to tell you," I interjected, a little angrily. "But now is different. Now I don't want to."

It probably wasn't the best thing to say to ease her concern. It was true, though. The box I'd packaged the night of the attack into, sealed tight, had burst open. I could think of nothing else. Only that outside was full of unknowns, of strangers who would cut you for money, boys who would never like you back, and shallow connections that would inevitably fade. I'd rather write about them than live amongst them.

Mum said, "You can talk to me about it," and waited a long time for me to talk about it. When I hit play on my laptop, she patted my leg and left the room.

I didn't hear them from upstairs. If I had, I wouldn't have come down. Especially not in my SpongeBob Squarepants pj's.

Mum was at the kitchen table and opposite her was Jenny Price, looking as prim and proper as ever. Jenny was the mother of Lauren Price–an old high school friend.

We hadn't maintained much contact, apart from one coffee catch up last year. Lauren was living out of home in a share house in Fitzroy, working at a café part time and spending the rest of her time paralytic drunk at music festivals. She had tatts now, and I could tell when we met up that she felt awkward about showing me. Even though I didn't really care, it was fairly obvious that what common ground we'd once shared had fallen out from under us.

Mum was still close with Jenny. So I got to hear about Lauren's life through the eyes of her fretful mother, and I'm sure she heard about mine through Mum. Although, my stories would be much less exciting than hers. Until now.

"Hello," Jenny trilled. "How are you, Dorothy?" It was a loaded question.

"I'm good, thanks." I smiled sweetly, hoping to disprove whatever Mum had been whispering to her before I walked in. Although, the SpongeBob pj's didn't help my credibility much, and neither did the fact that it was almost midday and I was still wearing them.

Despite all this, I tossed my hair back and strolled to the fridge, stepping over Kramer who was spread across the tiles. I pulled the water jug out–Dad insisted filtered water was better for us; I wasn't convinced–and poured myself a glass.

I saw they had cups of tea but offered them water anyway, just to emphasise my state of generosity and wellbeing.

"Your mother was just telling me about your ordeal," Jenny said. She had the sort of voice that grated on the ears, for the sole reason that it was so sickly sweet. I'd mentioned this to Mum, but she just told me not to be mean. That Jenny really was as sweet as she sounded. "How horrific. I always tell Lauren, be careful when you're alone at night, walking to your car or wherever you happen to be."

If Jenny knew all the places Lauren *happened to be* in her Instagram posts, she'd probably have a full-blown meltdown. It struck me then how unfair it all was.

It's not like I put myself in risky situations. I didn't often stay out late. I was conscious of parking my car in safe places. How was it that I was the one who became a target? The thought made me all kinds of bitter, but then I felt guilty for coming so close to wishing what happened to me upon someone else.

"Of course! I tell Dotty the same thing," Mum said. "Goes to show that sometimes you just can't predict these things." I could tell she was a little peeved by Jenny's comment too.

27

I'd come to the end of the journal, which meant I needed a new one. I knew if I asked Mum to buy it, she'd turn it into some milestone step I had to take for myself. *Come with me*, she'd say. *We'll pop down to the shops together.* And she'd get excited, because *maybe Dot is starting to feel better*.

But I wasn't, and I didn't want to go anywhere. So in the meantime I made do with loose sheets of lined paper I found around my room.

I stopped writing about what was and started writing about what could've been. Short stories, I guess. What-if stories. I wrote of the mugging, but changed the ending. A version where I didn't get my purse out in time, and another where Uncle Ray appeared with a bat to knock the guy senseless.

I wrote about the attacker—four different perspectives, all with varied reasons for doing what he did. Unless the police caught whoever it was, that person would remain anonymous to me. Maybe even forever. There was some relief in personifying him.

In some ways, it was like Flo sketching the boy who hadn't wanted her when she wanted him. In the devastation and the hurt, she could ease her inner turmoil by letting it slip onto paper. The only difference was that Flo knew Jesse. He had a face for her to draw.

My attacker didn't. And so I had to conjure him up from nothing. I was shaping him with rough sketches of possibility, but it was better than leaving him blank.

Since my head was such a chaotic mess, laying it all out took time. All I knew was that I didn't want it to end. I wanted to stay in my room, protected by its walls and alone in my thoughts forever.

That's why I was so jolted when Mum came in on Friday morning to tell me I had a visitor from Corner. Flo–I assumed.

She gave me this long, meaningful look before stepping aside to let someone through.

It wasn't Flo. It was *Jesse*. He walked in with his easy gait and hands in his pockets, as if he'd been here a thousand times before.

"Hey," he said, stopping a metre or so from my bed while I stashed my notepaper under the covers.

"Hi." I frowned at him. "This is a surprise."

Jesse nodded, like he agreed. "Yeah, there've been a few of those."

Silence held between us for a moment as I searched around for something to say. "How did you get my address?"

"I hacked into the work computer."

"Oh." A laugh stirred somewhere inside me, but not quite enough to reveal itself. "Well you can sit down, stalker." I gestured to my hand chair.

Jesse crossed the room and fell into it, the wheels squeaking as he swivelled side to side.

"I heard what happened," he said. "Obviously."

"Darcy told you?"

"Flo did."

"Oh. You two are talking?"

"Sort of." He shrugged. "What I meant was, you don't have to tell the story again."

I nodded. "Thanks."

Jesse cast his gaze about the room, his eyes slowing across my shelf of mementos. "Nice place."

"Why'd you come, then?" I posed, maybe a little brusquely. "If you already know."

His attention cut back to me and he started ruffling around in his inner jacket pockets. "To take a photo of you. You agreed to model for me, remember?" He pulled out a camera and I must have flinched, because his expression softened. "Kidding, kidding."

I continued eyeing the camera.

"Relax, I'm kidding," he said again. "I wanted to make sure you're all right."

I let loose a breath. "I'm still alive, aren't I?"

"Not the same thing." He shot me a wry smile. "Flo said you haven't been out of the house."

Oh, did she?

"I'm not sure why you came."

He laughed—a high-pitched chuckle. But his frown returned quickly. "Because you're scared. Aren't you?"

I considered the question—which was obviously more of a statement, given the inflection. If I tried to deny it, he wouldn't believe me anyway. So I shrugged, attempting to match his nonchalance. "A bit."

"Fair enough." He swung an arm back to hug one of the chair's red fingers. "The world is screwed up. It can feel better to stay out of it."

My hand went instinctively to my neck, and Jesse's eyes followed. He had a rare quality about him that elicited honesty. Probably because he was so honest himself. I felt some dark truths craning their necks, wanting to be seen. "The world is fine," I said. "It's people that are screwed up—that walk around doing horrible things." I took a breath and Jesse waited, still frowning. "It doesn't just feel scary to leave the house," I said. "It feels … impossible."

Jesse nodded, more somber than I had ever seen him. "Yeah, I understand that." Normally, when people said this, my first thought was—no, you don't. But somehow with Jesse, I believed it. His lips pressed together, and he made an agitated sound behind them.

At last, he said, "I've stolen before, you know."

"What do you mean?"

"I found a purse at work," he said. "I saw it fall from this lady's handbag, and I took it."

I blinked rapidly, awaiting elaboration.

"It was actually the reason Ray installed more security cameras, because the lady came back and requested we check them. But of course we only had one, and the angle didn't cover the relevant part of the restaurant."

"Okay …" I fiddled with the toggles of my hoodie, my eyes jumping between their frayed ends and Jesse's face. I got the impression I was the first to hear of this. Just like the truth about his sister Minty. What was it about me that made him comfortable enough to admit these things?

Jesse must have noted my surprise. "Yeah, probably not the smartest idea, telling the owner's niece, but anyway. I was in a bad place. My point is–nobody is pure good or pure bad. Not even me." He grinned, the lopsided way. "If we hid in our rooms because people are bad, we'd miss out on the good. If I didn't head down to the beach I'd never get photos of the sunset. That sounded lame, but you get me."

"Yeah." I did get him. At least, the logical part of my brain did. The other half didn't see anything wrong with hiding in my room for all eternity.

"Anyway, I was on my way into the city." He tapped his camera. "It's overcast today, good lighting. You can come if you want. Model for me."

"It's okay," I said, patting my doona down. "I've got some stuff to catch up on."

"I bet." Jesse rose, giving me a serious look. "I'll let you get back to it then." A small part of me considered asking about Flo and what they'd talked about. He paused at the door. "Come out sometime soon, though."

I nodded, and he left. I wanted to go with him. But although my cell had a window, I couldn't step outside. Not yet.

I considered calling after him, even as I heard the front door close.

———•———

Later that night my door creaked open. I was sitting on the hand chair reading Jodi Picoult. Dad appeared and threw something hard at me. It hit my shoulder and rolled to the floor.

"Ouch."

"Sorry." He sauntered inside while I bent to pick it up.

"*Honey and almond ice cream*," I read from the label. "*Coated in white chocolate and biscuit pieces.* Good one. Thanks Dad."

"Pleasure," he said, and a heavy sigh bent him at the knees till he was sitting at the end of my bed. When Mum wanted to talk she turned sharp, when Dad wanted to talk–everything drooped, from his posture to the cadence of his voice.

He twisted around. "I'm getting too old to crack backs that aren't mine."

"Take a holiday," I told him, not for the first time.

"Indeed I should."

I waited for it. *What's the matter? Why haven't you left the house? What can we do to help?* But instead he said, "Who was that fella who came around today?"

"Mum told you?"

Dad rested back on his elbows. "Of course she did." She'd probably sent him in here to collect information. I swore my Mum could work for the black ops.

"Jesse," I reluctantly offered. "He's just from Corner."

"Huh." He angled his head at the ceiling. "*Just from Corner.* I was convinced that young Liam Neeson kid would be the one to watch."

"He is," I said without thinking. "I mean, no. Neither of them are anything."

"Hm, okay." He didn't sound at all convinced, so I realised I'd need to well and truly nip it in the bud.

"Just friends." I drenched my tone with irrefutable finality. "Promise."

"Whatever you say, sweetie."

Ergh. The only-child curse–being the sole focal point for the spotlight. I lay my book over my chest and ripped into the ice cream.

"What else is new?" Dad asked as he looked around my room, and before I could answer he said, "What's that pepper doing up here?"

He knew just the wrong things to say. "It's a joke present from Darcy," I told him, and instantly wished I hadn't.

"A present from Darcy?"

"A *joke*," I rushed to clarify. "To defend myself, because you can't legally carry pepper spray in Australia."

"Is that right?" He looked puzzled. "I should look that up." Oh Dad. His expression suddenly twisted into bemusement. "Funny guy."

"Mhm." I took a bite of the ice cream and a shard of chocolate fell into my lap. I busied myself with retrieving it and scratching at the mark it left on my pj's. I heard Dad sigh and get to his feet.

"You can talk to me anytime, about anything," he said. "You know that don't you sweetie?"

"I know that," I answered. How could you tell someone who wanted to give you the world that you didn't really want it anymore?

FLO

I caught a bus to Em's at nine on Sunday morning. She'd drive us both from there. I couldn't be sure how Dot would react, but after Jesse's text on Friday, I thought I'd take a risk.

Jesse: *Just saw Dot. You should go see her too.*

I might've been surprised to hear he'd visited her, although I'd also stopped trying to predict what Jesse may or may not do.

I could sense that he liked Dot, and although I'd been skeptical at times, I was fairly sure now that it wasn't a romantic interest.

A couple of days after Dot told me about Minty, I messaged him asking if he wanted to get dins Thursday night. I did this on a Tuesday, when I knew he wasn't working so I wouldn't have to face him. I tried to set my expectations low, but when he took a full day to reply I got super nervous. It turned out okay, though, 'cos his answer was yes.

We went to *The Melt* between our houses–he picked me up–and ordered this metre long pizza at Jesse's insistence. I was convinced we wouldn't finish it, but he powered through to the last crust.

He was funny like that, Jesse. If you said something was impossible, he'd always try to prove you wrong, even if it really was. *That fence is way too high to climb.* And off he'd go. *I can't carry four plates at a time.* And he'd lay them on me. It had been months since we'd spent that much time together, and I realised pretty quickly how I missed his optimism … or maybe it was defiance. Either way, I missed it.

At our cars, he'd gone quiet. I didn't try to fill the silence though, 'cos I sensed he had something to say and I was scared that if I butted in, he might never say it.

"I'm really sorry Flo," he'd said without looking at me. "I should never have let you think …"

I didn't want to hear about how I'd been led on by him, or how much he regretted what happened between us. "I appreciate that," I said quickly. "I regret it too, but it's in the past."

He looked up, a little confused. "I never said I regretted it."

"Well." I shrugged. "Don't you?"

Jesse drove his focus into slowly kicking the concrete. "Aspects of it. But–it's really complicated."

I knew that much, now that I knew about Minty. We didn't speak about her the entire night and hadn't since. I didn't think that mattered though. Like Dot said, he wanted me to *know*. Talking it out wasn't the point, unless he wanted it to be. I'd reached out. He'd apologised. That was enough for now.

I texted Em when I was out the front, mainly 'cos I was absolutely terrified of her pit bull, Merry. He wasn't as friendly as his name made him sound, let me tell you.

I caught a glimpse of his big, ogre head in the lounge room window and shuddered to myself. Em appeared moments later, bustling down the garden path with a picnic rug tucked under her arm.

Either side of the garden was chock-full of weeds and the grass needed a mow like two months ago. I hated that I noticed things like that. I blamed it on my parents. Their obsession with gardening must've translated to a subconscious awareness in me. I knew what Dad would say, too.

"The soil is a stage. When you plant a bulb, you gotta ensure the best lighting and the best set dressing. You're the director and the show rests on your shoulders."

I'd heard him use it as a sort of pitch over the phone for clients interested in his services. I never knew whether to cringe or smile. Usually I did both.

"You got the goods?" Em locked the front gate behind her and spun to me. She always looked a little wild–hair frazzled and carefree–like she'd either just got off a rollercoaster or was about to step onto one.

I wiggled the bag I was holding in her face. It was full of cheese and crackers and berries I'd bought on my way.

"I'll transfer you money," she said, wielding her keys as she led me to her car.

"That's okay." I'd thought of the idea, so I was happy to cover it. Corner wages weren't immense, but they were enough for emergencies like these.

Em chatted away for most of the drive, which made me think about Dot and how I liked that she didn't have this compulsive need to fill silence. Although, Em was good value most of the time. She brought warmth and humour, and I had a feeling Dot was in need of both.

When we knocked on her door, I started to wonder if we should've come at all. I liked my privacy. I was fairly sure Dot did too and we understood each other on that level. But here I was, barging into her home, knowing full well she hadn't left it in weeks and *why* would now be any different? 'Cos I brought Em to peer pressure her into it? Crap. This was far from ideal.

Before I could swivel away, the front door opened wide to reveal a skinny lady in a singlet and a loose, floral skirt. She looked perplexed to see us on her doorstep, and I couldn't blame her for it.

"Hi there." Em took the lead, reaching to shake her hand. "We're friends of Dot."

The lady had a young face aside from the lines between her brows and around her mouth. Her hair was dyed golden blonde with dark roots showing through. I could tell she would've been a stunner back in the day. "Friends of Dot," she repeated, frowning a little. "Does she know you're coming?"

"Nope." Em grinned, and I stepped forward to soften her cheeky ambiguity.

"We work at Corner together," I explained, "and we thought we'd just drop in."

The lady smiled, and suddenly I registered the family resemblance. It was a mildly uncertain bend of humour I'd seen Dot wear many times before–a smile that didn't quite know what it was doing, or how long it should stay.

"I'm Kat, Dot's Mum." She opened the door a little wider and beckoned us inside before we could offer our names. "Forgive the mess," she said, gesturing at piles of Tupperware and glasses on the table. "We're in the middle of a spring clean. Well, it's summer now, isn't it? Anyway. Have a seat girls, I'll just go check on her."

Em trotted into the lounge room and collapsed into the biggest chair. I perched on its armrest.

"So you saw Jesse Thursday night?" Em said out of nowhere.

I tried to mask my shock. My Dad always said I wasn't very good at hiding how I felt. Apparently I had Mum's eyes–they gave everything away. Willing them into an ordinary degree of alertness, I asked, "Where'd you hear that?"

"I overheard Jesse telling Darcy last night at work."

"It wasn't a big deal," I said, trying not to think what it might mean that Jesse would tell Darcy. "We were both free so we went for pizza."

"You haven't done that since awards night." Em knew about awards night. Everyone seemed to know about it.

I shrugged. "Well it doesn't mean anything. We're just reconnecting, as friends."

"Uh-huh." Em made no effort to hide her skepticism. I pretended I couldn't hear it though. And luckily, that was when Dot appeared.

"Holy moly," Em said. "You look like hell, gal."

Dot was stricken, glancing from me to Em and back to me, like I was the one who could explain what was going on. She'd always had a thin frame, but now it was even thinner. Her hair, which was so short it didn't even graze her shoulders, was half up and half down, and her cheeks were corpse-pale.

"I–what are you two doing here?" she said. Her voice was scratchy, as though she'd just woken up or hadn't used it in a while. Either way–in combination with the rest of her–I was worried.

"We're bringing you a picnic," Em said. "And, maybe some sun if you'll let us take you out, Count Dracula."

It was insensitive and I cringed, but Dot smiled, albeit reluctantly. It disappeared though, when Em added, "We heard about your car park episode. What a nightmare!"

Dot cut her gaze to me, and I clarified quickly. "Ray told everyone what happened," I said. "He thought it was important we all knew, so no one would walk to their cars alone."

"Makes sense," Dot muttered. She dug her teeth into her bottom lip. I noticed she did that a lot when we first met, but much less as time went by. You could tell that conversations with strangers made her nervous, and the lip chewing might have come from her reluctance to say what she thought. Only, she'd come to speak quite openly since, at least with me. So I hadn't seen her do it in a while. I didn't like that she was doing it now.

"You really didn't have to do this," she said.

Em leapt to her feet. "Where should we go?"

I could tell, looking at Dot's face, just how little she wanted to *go* anywhere. She'd told me over text that leaving the house was hard. Why had I thought that a picnic rug and some crackers would change that?

Before the silence could drag much longer, I tugged on a thread of inspiration and said, "Do you have a backyard?"

29

It was easy to forget how lovely the sun was until I felt it again, the warmth pulsing under my skin. The picnic rug Emma brought was only small so we sat huddled together, our knees touching around the snacks between us. I wasn't hungry. Emma was though. This was her lunch, we were told, as she scooped avocado dip onto a cracker and topped it with a wedge of Brie cheese.

I knew how pathetic I must have seemed–all cooped up in my lazy trackies, a size too small but soft as anything, brought out of my hole like some traumatized animal. It was such a contrast to Flo's clean white sandals, denim shorts frayed the perfect amount, her hair pulled back neatly into that elegant, swishing ponytail. Every part of her seemed so effortless.

I'd barely had time to look in a mirror, so God only knew what the girls were seeing. My hair was so short that if I didn't style it, it looked more like a bird's nest. But I didn't really care. Once the rug was set up and we were talking about things that weren't me, I was glad they'd come.

"Flo was just telling me about her date with Jesse," Emma said, her mouth full of food.

Flo gasped while I cut a look to her. We hadn't texted about the Jesse situation. Mostly just about me. My journal. I had told her how trapped I felt in my head, and how the writing alleviated that just enough to keep me sane. How I was starting to want to leave the house, but couldn't overcome the darker thoughts to stay inside it.

And what had I asked about her life? I felt a sudden shame grip me and I turned to the platter to hide it, picking out a fat strawberry.

"It wasn't a date, Em," Flo muttered through a sigh. Then she looked at me. "It wasn't a date. We just caught up for dins on Thursday. Super casual."

"I bet." Emma winked at me with her whole face. But I believed Flo. She was giving me such an earnest stare that I had no choice but to believe her.

If Emma wasn't there I would have asked if the dinner happened because of the Minty revelation, but I was fairly certain Emma didn't know anything about it and that if she did find out, pretty soon everyone else would too. So I asked trivial questions like *where'd you go* and *what did you eat*?

"Did you kiss?" Emma chimed in, receiving a withering stare from Flo.

We went on to talk about silly things, little things. But somehow those little things were big enough to override everything that had kept me in the dark all those weeks. Just for a little while. Granted I was only in my backyard, but I was still out of the house, and happy to be.

30

We were having roast chicken and veggies for dinner when Dad dropped, "So I was talking to Terry at work today—he has this friend who's a psychologist, and apparently she's fantastic."

I glanced at Mum. She hadn't looked up, which meant this conversation had been carefully engineered. That fact alone bothered me, so I wasn't going to make this easy for them. I shovelled potato into my mouth.

Dad cleared his throat. I could see him looking at me in my periphery, but I stared at my plate and waited.

"Dot," he said at last. "We could arrange for her to come around if you'd like."

"Mhm."

"What do you say to that? It could be interesting, even just to meet her. She sounds like a real character."

I swallowed my mouthful and finally looked across at him. It's not like I could pretend nothing was wrong—I was still wearing last night's pjs. My credibility was at an all-time low.

I knew Dad was making an effort to play it down. But even if he'd sat me down and said *your mother and I think you need to see a psychologist*, the meaning was the same. I needed help. Help that not even Dad or Mum felt equipped to offer. That realisation alone made me heavy enough to sink through the floor.

The feeling must have surfaced in my expression, because Dad got up from his chair and came around to mine. He squeezed my head into his shoulder while I blinked furiously to bat away tears. It was only when Mum reached across the table to grip my arm that they fell.

"Dorothy," Dad said. "You're too precious. Too precious to stay hidden away, sweetie."

Mum didn't cry often—it was normally Dad who unleashed his emotion at the drop of a hat—but I could see her swiping under her eyes.

And then it was easy, to nod and say, "Okay," because me hurting was one thing, but them hurting because of me was another.

———◆———

Dad was right—she was a real character. Doctor Reem was her name. He suggested she could meet me in my room, but I didn't want that. She was still a stranger after all, a stranger I was about to welcome into my mind. The least she could do was stay out of my room. So I made sure I was downstairs by three.

I'd thrown on my favourite hoodie for the occasion–it had NEW YORK embroidered across it, even though I'd never been–and I even slid myself into jeans.

It struck me then that Doctor Reem couldn't know I'd been wearing pjs and trackies for almost a month straight. That you could make yourself appear as anything if you put enough effort into the illusion.

I was thinking about this when Dad let her inside. He'd taken a day off breaking backs so he could be around while she was here, even though Mum already was too. I had strictly told them both that I'd be furious if I caught them eavesdropping, which was something they would possibly definitely try to do. I even made them pinky promise they'd stay upstairs.

Doctor Reem was wide and short and wore square, silver frames that made her eyes look enormous. Maybe they gave her x-ray vision so that she could see right through you to sort out your problems more easily.

Once Dad had finished his bout of small talk at the door, he came in and said, "Oh, this is my daughter, Dorothy," as if I wasn't the whole reason she was here. Doctor Reem smiled, showing a gap between her front teeth, and shook my hand. Hers was firm and warm.

"The Dinosaur?" she said. It wasn't the first time I'd heard this joke, but I forced a smile anyway.

"She's named after me," I replied, not for the first time either.

Dad laughed too loud and motioned for us to sit on the couches. Then he muttered something about herbal tea and left.

"So." Doctor Reem dropped her bag by her feet. I wondered if it had a notebook inside, or a computer, or something else that could fix me. "Your father told me what happened last month. You're brave, Dorothy. I know it already."

I laughed, because no I wasn't. "How do you know?"

"Because you let me visit you!" Doctor Reem sunk back into the couch. She looked about Mum's age. I started wondering if she had kids, and if they were the victims of constant psychoanalysis. I bet they weren't cripplingly anxious their whole lives, like me. "Tell me more about all that is Dorothy," Doctor Reem said.

I rattled off the bare essentials–I was studying Business at Swinburne, working at my uncle's restaurant, had started writing recently and was enjoying that … Doctor Reem stopped me there, like she could sense the subject matter. Maybe it was obvious—since I realised I was wringing my hands at that point.

"What do you write about?"

I hesitated. *I can be anything*, I thought again, *if I put enough effort into the illusion*. But I didn't feel like putting in effort. I was tired. Empty. So I just said, "Lots of things. Mostly the attack."

Dad sauntered in with two cups of tea, laying them on the coffee table between us.

"Thanks Dad," I said with a pointed look. He only lingered a second longer before clapping his hands together and disappearing upstairs. Hopefully he would stay there.

Doctor Reem was nodding, pensively, and I realised then how much she resembled a wise, old owl in specs. Like a character from a storybook. Her eyes were a bright shade too, closer to amber than brown. She asked me to tell her more about the attack, so I did.

I tried to ignore the pounding of my heart and the way my hands became damp while I recounted leaving Corner, the confrontation, falling, climbing into my car, a friend finding me there.

As I spoke, Doctor Reem reached for her mug and blew over the tea, taking careful sips. For some reason, that eased my nerves and I could speak more freely. Maybe she was a witchdoctor undercover.

She asked me if I recalled the night vividly. I said yes. She asked whether it affected my sleep. Yes.

Then she asked if I felt nervous leaving the house because of it, and I said sometimes, which really meant yes.

Doctor Reem told me this was unsurprising— that twenty-five percent of people experienced varying degrees of post-traumatic stress after similar ordeals or events. That there was no *correct* way to respond. That everyone was different, and I shouldn't be ashamed of how I was feeling.

This turned my stomach into a knot, because how could she tell I was ashamed? Was I that transparent, or was she that clever?

She asked what I wanted, and I answered with what I didn't. "I don't want to be scared anymore." It sounded lame out loud, but it was the closest I could get to a succinct truth.

Doctor Reem didn't treat it like a lame admission. She told me I was *impressively self-aware*, and that we could work on this. That I would be okay. Things would get better. Easier.

I hadn't expected to readily admit so much, especially not to a perfect stranger. But ironically, it seemed to be Doctor Reem's *strangeness* that gave me the courage. I understood then more profoundly why Jesse might have felt compelled to tell me about Minty's death.

If you were almost ready to share and then encountered someone open to hearing you, someone who knew you just enough but not too much–the stars could align. They could light you up with such clarity that hiding seemed pointless, and the only thing left to do was admit who you were before the stars went on their way and you were lost in the dark again.

By the time I remembered my tea and took a sip, it was cold. How long had we been talking?

Three hours, Dad told me when she left. We'd spoken for three hours. He said he was proud of me and hugged me tight.

I felt a rush of love for him and for Mum, who could be proud of the smallest step, even if it wasn't beyond the front door.

31

I ran my fingers over the rows of cards, three by nine. Half of them were from places I'd been with Cameron. Others he'd collected for me and passed on.

I started sifting through the pages and pulled out cards from the places I'd never been. There wasn't much point in keeping those. I had no memories associated with them and no desire to change that.

Mum called me a *serial hoarder*, but I didn't think it was so easy to define. I applied meaning to things because I craved meaning in things. At the heart of the hoarding, I collected what I lacked.

I came to the final page of my business cards and hesitated. The last I'd added was from *Jesse Melrose - Photographer*. I recalled Reese's party, and although it wasn't long ago, it felt far away. Buried. Our conversation bubbled to the forefront of my mind. Jesse sharing his sister's death with me. Minty. It was a cute nickname.

A churning sadness swam inside me and I let the folder slip. There was so much to despise about the world. If it wasn't humanity itself, it was sickness. Disease. Violence. Bad things happening to innocent people who pulled the short straws.

If anger was my overwhelming emotion, maybe I could still function. But it wasn't—everything rode on fear. *Fear* of the people and the sickness and the violence. It was debilitating in a way nothing else could be. And more than anything I hated myself for letting it break me down, while people like Jesse Melrose walked through hell and made it back without dissolving into trembling messes on their bedroom floors.

———•———

During Doctor Reem's third visit, I brought out my journal and the scrambled notepaper that followed. Handing it to her felt like delivering my brain on a platter, disconnecting from some inner sanctum of myself. But I was lighter without it.

She flipped through the pages, those amber eyes raking over the words as she asked sporadic questions about what I'd written.

"You mention here that you don't like yourself," she said, holding my book in one hand and her chamomile tea in the other. "That you didn't even before the attack."

"Mmm." I thought on it. Doctor Reem always gave me ample time to think, as if she knew how long it would take for the honest answer to reveal itself. "I've always felt nervous," I admitted. "My ex used to tease me about how I hated interacting with people I didn't know. He'd call me the Grinch and I told myself it was funny." But it wasn't. Because other people weren't the problem–I was. "I mean, I do like getting to know people. I just don't know how to do it without the panic. So it's easier to avoid altogether."

Doctor Reem put my journal on the coffee table and tapped her mug with a fingernail. "You've taken a job at a restaurant," she said. "What made you choose to do that?"

"Family obligation," I answered. "It's my uncle's and he needed a waitress, so Mum volunteered me."

"You don't think you might have *wanted* to step into a non-intimidating space where you could connect with people?"

I laughed. "I wouldn't call waitressing non-intimidating."

"Well, it's a job that requires social interaction in short stints." Which was my idea of hell, I felt like saying. "Did you find it helped with your anxiety at all? Before the attack?"

"Uh …" I paused to take a sip of grape juice from my cup and give myself more time to consider. I hadn't thought much about how Corner had helped me. The attack was overpowering and seemed to erase any progress I might have been making before it. "I guess, yeah. At the start I absolutely hated approaching tables. But it got easier over time." And I *had* made connections, however incidental–connections with people who wanted to invite me for kebabs and ice cream and sleepovers. That realisation alone made a dormant light in me flicker to life. Maybe I wasn't as alone in my cage as I'd come to believe.

———•———

A day later Flo texted asking if I wanted to go for a *little* walk. I was positive the word *little* was bound to a strategy–one that would loosen the leash on the anxiety keeping me attached to the house.

But I agreed, and we walked and talked about Jesse and how she had finally told him she knew about Minty, and that Darcy and Nina were apparently on the rocks because he was starting to realise *what a cow* she was–Flo's words, not mine. It felt good to talk about normal things.

We were two streets away when I started to fade. I couldn't seem to retain Flo's words. The leash was pulling on my neck, choking me. I asked her to repeat herself a bunch of times before she eventually said, "Let's go back."

And as we got closer to home, the leash loosened again. I hated it. I wanted to slash it away but it was thick and unbreakable.

I told Doctor Reem about my metaphorical leash during our fourth meeting. She said I should stop trying to hack at it and instead, try to stretch it. Ease myself further away without fear of what would happen if it were to break. That made sense to me.

So I went with Mum to get groceries Monday morning. I stayed in the car, but I still went.

On Wednesday, Flo, Emma and I had fish and chips on the beach down at Elwood. Emma drove us and played Disney Classics the entire way. She knew almost every word of every song.

It didn't surprise me that Emma loved Disney. She was practically a Disney character herself.

Flo told us that Darcy and Nina had broken up. "About time," Emma said.

A month ago, I might have been glad to hear it. Now it didn't seem to matter. Not in the grand scheme of things.

Darcy had sent me three texts over the past few weeks, *just checking in*, he'd said in one of them, but I hadn't responded to any. Maybe I was still mad he'd told Nina about the attack. Or maybe since I was using up all my emotional energy on myself, I had nothing left to spare for him.

I could see why Jesse might've rejected Flo when he did, even if he liked her at the time. When your state of mind was muddled and broken, it took all your strength to deal with it. Heal it. Factoring in another person felt like adding to the mess, spreading it out rather than mopping it up.

I didn't go to the beach often, not even on a good day. I hated the sand, how it got caught in the towel and my fingernails and even on our fish and chips. But the water was mesmerising. Sweeping close, pulling back. Glittering.

Near. Far. Repeat. I saw myself in it. The motion was predictable, but what it brought onto the shore wasn't. I collected a piece of dried coral and a cream, spiral shell flecked with purple.

For my next session with Doctor Reem, she suggested we meet at her office. It was only ten minutes away, even closer than the beach had been. So I agreed, and on Friday afternoon Dad drove me there.

We spoke about my progress and I showed her the spiral shell, which I had kept in my pocket since the beach day.

Back in primary school we were given opportunities to show-and-tell, to bring in an object, inanimate or living, and tell the class about it. It was my favourite part of class. Every kid would crane their neck and stare at whatever you'd brought along like it was the most precious thing in the world, even if it was just a rubber bouncy ball or one of those metal slinkies.

It didn't matter what it was, what mattered was that it was something you'd brought in from another place.

The shell rested in my palm, and as Doctor Reem bent forward to inspect it, grinning ear to ear, I felt the same proud flutter that I once had during show-and-tell. It didn't matter what it was. What mattered was that I'd brought it in from another place.

32

I was ready. Mum had even ironed the apron. My nerves were in full swing, but not panicked. They were moving slowly, making my fingers tingle and my heart beat louder in my ears. It was a bustling sort of excitement. I was going back to Corner.

Uncle Ray had been telling us about an upcoming training day at dinner. All the dubs were attending. Apparently there had been a few changes to the menu, and so he'd decided to run the staff through it alongside a recap of Corner's values and processes.

"Can I come?" The words were out before I could overthink them. Everyone looked dumbfounded, particularly Mum and Dad.

It had been almost two months since I'd been to Corner, and I'd shown zero interest in going back. I'd felt it, though. Mostly because I missed working with Flo and Emma and Jesse, and—dare I say it—Darcy.

"Don't know why you'd want to ..." Peter muttered into his wine glass.

"Of course!" Uncle Ray just about turned the table over. "Of course you can. We've suffered without you, girl. Oh how we've suffered."

———◆———

I sat in my car and stared out the window, tracing the spaces that had plagued my every thought the past two months. I couldn't say for sure, but I vaguely knew where it was that he'd rushed at me, and where I'd fallen.

It felt far away and close at the same time. Sharp in some places and hazy in others.

A lone figure snagged my attention, strolling gracefully toward the Corner door with her ponytail dancing in the breeze behind her. I leapt out of my car and dashed across the car park. It would be nice to walk in with someone, rather than brave it alone.

"Oh!" Flo halted when she saw me coming at her. I must've looked like a mad woman, keys rattling and backpack bouncing against my shoulder.

"Hey," I said when I reached the top stair, taking a few deep breaths to disguise my frenzy.

"Hello there." Flo looked like she was trying not to smile, but then she did anyway. "I didn't expect to see you."

I gave a rapid shrug. "It was a last-minute thing."

"The best kind," she said. And then she stepped forward to give me a firm hug.

I relaxed. It was as if she was conducting the perfect mix of energy and calm right through me and I could take on the world so long as I could retain it. Or, at least, hold myself together for the next couple of hours.

Flo hesitated with her hand on the door. "I have something for you by the way," she said. "If I'd known you were coming I would've brought it."

"Oh. You didn't have to get me—"

"No, no, don't get excited. It's just a small gift." Before I could question her more she pushed on the door. I followed after her, momentarily distracted by the mention of this *small gift*—enough that I forgot to feel daunted by the group waiting inside. That is until I saw them there, sitting in a wide semi-circle. Most heads whipped toward us as we approached.

The restaurant was cool compared to the hot afternoon outside, which made me shiver. Or maybe it was just my skittering nerves.

Uncle Ray had closed Corner for training, so everyone was wearing casual clothes. I ran my gaze quickly across the few kitchen staff I recognised, including the bald man who locked me in the fridge, Reese and Emma, a couple of unfamiliar faces, Jude, Jesse, and then Darcy, who was sitting nearest the door. My heart burst into a gallop.

I wondered if he was also thinking back to the last time we'd seen each other. When I'd had to run to the bathroom after meeting his girlfriend. I wondered if he even knew what Nina had said that night, whether she'd asked him why the weird girl at Corner couldn't string two words together.

Uncle Ray was standing in front of everyone with Jude close behind, beaming across at us.

"Join, join," he said, ushering us in. Flo dragged two chairs beside Darcy and sat in the one furthest away. I inwardly rolled my eyes and dropped into the other, right beside him.

I gritted my teeth and forced myself to look left and smile. Jesse flicked two fingers in greeting. Darcy smiled back, full and warm but a little uncertain.

"Everyone's here!" Emma said, grinning ear to ear.

Jude handed me and Flo sheets of laminated paper, the same that everyone else appeared to be holding.

Uncle Ray gave me a quick wink before clapping his hands together. "I'll try to make this as painless as possible, because I'm aware that most of you lot already know how things go here. So just think of this as a refresher course, kids."

Reese's hand shot up as if he were in fact a kid at school. "Do we get paid for this?"

"I was wondering how soon one of you would ask that," muttered Jude.

"Yes," Uncle Ray confirmed. "If you behave."

Reese shot Emma a pointed look and she poked him in the side so hard he arched away and almost fell off his chair. Jesse grabbed him before he could.

My gaze dropped to the menu in my hands. I skimmed over each new item as Uncle Ray started a spiel on the history of the Corner chain. It was one I'd heard a thousand times before, probably a lot more than the rest of the group had.

I wanted to establish a place where customers wouldn't feel like customers, but guests. Or even better—family. Coming into Corner should feel like coming home ... It would sound lame if he wasn't so genuine about it all.

"Hey." Darcy's whisper shocked me back to attention. He glanced sidelong at me. "Where've you been, Dot?"

I chewed my lip and sifted through a number of mildly humorous responses before settling on, "Just in my room." It could have been funny, if it weren't so true.

"You kinda fell off the map," he whispered, and actually sounded mildly concerned about it. "Left me to tackle the deadly Saturday shifts on my own."

Poor you, I wanted to say. But that might have been overdoing it. So instead I just shrugged. It wasn't really the time and place to bring up the night of the attack, or that I was still bitter he'd told his girlfriend about it and she'd raised it with me like it was no more significant than someone snagging my lunch.

I tried to fashion an invisible, impenetrable wall between me and Darcy so that I could tune into Uncle Ray's speech again. He was like Mum–animated and articulate, commanding attention with carefully timed highs and lows.

Mum was more reserved than Uncle Ray, but public speaking came naturally to both of them and I envied that. I'd received Dad's blustery, stuttering gene, which was sometimes endearing, but mostly just unimpressive.

As time rolled on and Uncle Ray started covering customer complaints, the wall I'd constructed started to fizzle. Darcy's cologne was woody and fresh. Whiffs of vanilla and ginger swam from my nose up into my head where they insisted on reminding me how close we were sitting. I angled my face away from him in a vain attempt to forget.

But then I somehow caught a glimpse of his black Adidas shoes. They matched the hoodie he was wearing with its black-and-white toggles. I wondered if that was intentional. Darcy always seemed well put together, but there was only so much you could infer from the standard Corner uniform and whatever was thrown on over it.

Beside him, Jesse's pale knees were showing through rips in his jeans, and he was wearing a pair of Vans that looked centuries old.

Then I was thinking about how the outside reflected the inside. Was clothing or hair or make-up indicative of anything at all? How many assumptions could you make based on what you could gather with your eyes alone? I gripped my arms and wondered about my choice for the day and what it might say about me–a loose, yellow tee with faded, blue jeans and white runners.

What if I'd chosen shorts and a singlet like Flo, or a bright, tee shirt dress like Emma?

I thought of Flo's paintings and the blatant vulnerability of them. She could paint whatever she wanted–she was good enough. But she painted what she felt most strongly and the art was better for it.

We were like canvases too, in a way. We layered ourselves with colour and patterns and smiles but it wasn't always honest. Maybe if it was, we'd be better for it too.

33

After an hour in Corner, Uncle Ray led us out into the car park. There was a minibus waiting there. We climbed in while he held the door open with this smug smile that scared me out of my wits.

Flo and I sat in the front seat where I could pester Uncle Ray about where we were headed. The third time I asked he zipped his lips and actually opened the van window to throw the key outside. I knew it was irretrievable. He could be stubborn, just like Mum.

Jude gripped Uncle Ray's shoulder as he swung himself up the stairs to sit by the driver.

I'd grown to like Jude. He was sassy and scarily candid at times, but also thoughtful and patient. It was a combination that left you feeling like he might be skeptical of your shortcomings, but still happy to solve the problems they posed without batting an eyelid.

When the bowling alley came into view, I considered making a run for it. I despised bowling and really couldn't understand why anyone would enjoy it.

The shoes were always horrendous and sweaty and the sizing was never right. All eyes were on you while you sauntered to the lane only to slip and slide your way into an uncoordinated attempt at throwing the ball. The game dragged on and on, and for some reason, just when you thought it was over—there was always another bonus game to follow, even if you'd only paid for one. What was with that?

I sighed as we moved inside. Uncle Ray clapped me on the back. "I used to bring you here, remember?" he said. "You and Peter, when you were little tackers."

Unfortunately, I did remember. I also remembered the countless parties at the bowling alley I'd been forced by friends into attending, all throughout primary school. Even high school.

Jesse came up beside me. "Little tackers, hey?" His brows lifted high. "So you must be pro then, if you've been bowling since then." I glared at him, just as Flo appeared at my other side.

"Well you can expect her to be better than you," she mused. "Remember awards night two years back?"

"Oi." Jesse shook his head at her. "Let's not."

"He ran too far," Flo told me, already laughing, "slipped on the lane and fell on his bum." I rarely heard her so hysterical, and that made me laugh just as much as the story did.

"It's fun," Jesse said, frankly. "You should try it sometime."

The lanes were all empty. Surprise, surprise. Nobody else thought the bowling alley was the place to be.

I tried to ask the lady for my shoe size in a hushed voice, because my feet were unusually small for someone of my age and stage, but she repeated it back at megaphone volume. Trust.

I found an empty bench and started on the laces. When I was onto the second shoe, Emma plonked herself down beside me. "Hey girl. It's good to see you." If anyone else had said it, it might have sounded forced, or even sympathetic. But it was Emma. Nothing woeful ever came out of her mouth. Despite her loud and occasionally obnoxious calls, I liked that about her.

"Good to see you too," I said.

"I hate these freaking shoes," she muttered, battling with the knotted laces. "Who decided bowling shoes would be red and black and ugly anyway?"

Probably the same person who decided bowling would be a fun idea.

Emma yanked the laces tight, and then looked around. "You can actually tell a lot about someone from their shoes."

I tucked my white runners under my arm, but she'd already spotted them. "Like, for example—white shoes generally indicate a certain level of douchiness." My face must have fallen a little, because she burst out laughing. "But that only applies to *guys*. If a girl has spanking-clean white shoes, it means she can be trusted. If a guy has the same spanking-clean white shoes–run. The whiter the shoe, the dirtier the mind."

"Interesting."

Emma gave a sage nod. "It's a true thing."

I didn't point out that Reese's shoes were the whitest in the room.

The game started off just as painfully as I anticipated, mostly due to that nasty bully in my head trying to tell me how stupid I looked every time I went to bowl. But as the night went on, the voice eased away. Emma would shriek and groan and cause a general ruckus after every go, which was funny and distracting. And miraculously–I even hit a few pins down.

The times the ball slid right down the gutter, Jesse would give me a high-five on my return, which was very likely just a dig at my pathetic aim, but I appreciated it regardless.

I wasn't even the worst there. Emma's run to the lane was a hurried shuffle, and when she threw the ball it was always too high with a booming landing. Flo's technique was delicate but direct. The ball slid down the lane at a snail's pace, generally meeting a couple of pins.

I tried not to look when it was Darcy's turn. He was great, naturally. His leg would slide back like a dancer's, sometimes even in time with the loud music blaring from the speakers, and the ball would shoot off with the perfect degree of power.

But that wasn't what got to me. It was his return to the group. If it were a strike he'd whip around and smile—a smile that refused to spread in full so as not to appear too bigheaded. And then often he'd do something silly like poke Jesse's nose or tousle Reese's hair. On one dodgy turn he turned and looked at me with this adorable, cringe face.

Okay, I still liked him. I liked him way too much. And that's why it still hurt that he'd spread my secret. It also didn't help that his break-up with Nina was so fresh. She and I were like chalk and cheese. Where she was curvy length I was short and narrow, and where she had silky hair the colour of dark chocolate, mine was thick and unruly and didn't even touch my shoulders.

The main Corner chef—whose name was Oli, I finally discovered—won the game, with Uncle Ray second and Darcy coming in third.

We got back in the van and headed back to the restaurant. Everyone stood around talking for a good half-hour, before Flo took my arm and asked if I could drop her home so she could give me the gift she'd mentioned earlier.

She announced our leave, thankfully, and we turned to go. I couldn't help but throw a casual glance in Darcy's direction. He was watching me, but averted his eyes fast.

I fought a smile on my way out.

Flo's parents were sitting on the couch under her vibrant sunset painting. Her Dad was reading a *Better Homes and Gardens* magazine and her Mum was knitting. I took a mental picture of the scene, because it was so lovely.

"This is Dorothy, Mum," Flo announced. "Dad, you've met."

Her mother didn't stop knitting, but she looked up and said, "Hello there, aren't you a pretty girl." I could see where Flo inherited her wide, sky-blue eyes.

"Mum, please," she muttered.

"What did I do?"

"Don't be creepy."

"But she is pretty! I can't point it out?"

Flo sighed while I blushed and soon enough I was swept down the hall into her bedroom. It was a little cleaner since I'd last seen it. There were fewer canvases. Less stray paint.

"Sorry about Mum," Flo said. "She seems to think compliments have no boundaries."

I stifled a laugh. "It's okay. I think she's pretty too."

Flo shot me a wry smile before moving for the easel by the window. There was a paint-flecked sheet draped over it. "Alrighty, close your eyes."

I obeyed, fighting the temptation to squint. I hated surprises. Once, my parents organised a surprise party for me and invited all my school friends to the house. I was coming home from my clarinet lesson at the time. When Dad opened the door and everyone shouted *SURPRISE!* I flung my clarinet case across the room and it hit Teresa Porter in the head. There was blood, and soon after, a giant egg protruding from her temple. She cried most of the night before her Mum picked her up. Let's just say that was the last surprise party ever thrown in my honour, and the last time Teresa spoke to me.

"Open."

Flo was sitting on the edge of her bed with a large canvas set across her knees. I didn't recognise the design immediately, because it was so different now. The left side was swallowed by black paint, thick and unyielding. The other half was full of whorls and swirls of brilliant colour–pinks and oranges and blues and yellows. A girl was painted from behind in the centre. She was standing on the black side, peering around into the colour.

Flo gripped its edges a little tighter. "Do you like it?"

"It's …" I couldn't settle on a word that did it justice.

"I'm calling it–*Corner*," Flo said, finally looking up with a slightly sheepish smirk. "I thought of the idea at work one night, before I even met you. I was on coffees and all the dubs were coming into the kitchen, yelling *'corner', 'corner'*, you know. But the painting only came to me after what happened with you."

I stared at her, tears standing still in my eyes.

"I thought it worked on multiple levels. Like, you can stay in the darkness, if you choose to, but that way you miss out on all the colour. Know what I mean?"

My throat was tight. I swallowed and nodded, then came closer to get a better look. The girl had cropped hair like mine. She was wearing an apron, its ribbon tied at her back.

The more I looked at the canvas the more of myself I saw, and not just in the girl. In the plain, black strokes. It was the darkest night and the stars covered over. It was my cheek against asphalt and the shadow of a man I'd never know.

I saw myself in the colour too. I saw Dad and Mum. Uncle Ray and Doctor Reem. The beach and its waves and all the shells passed up to us like little treasures in the sand. I saw Flo, Emma, Jesse, and Darcy.

I saw the nothing and I saw the everything. They existed side by side, divided by a single line. It was only while standing there in Flo's room looking at both halves that I realised how fine that line was.

35

Uncle Ray told me to come in early for my shift on Saturday. We were hanging Christmas decorations, since it was now December. Darcy and Flo were already at it by the time I got there. They were stringing fairy lights above the tables, standing on ladders to wind them around the timber beams in the ceiling. *Glass Animals* was blasting from the speakers so loudly they didn't even notice I'd come in until I was standing right underneath Flo's ladder.

"Hi!" Her face lit up and I smiled back.

"Need a hand?"

"Hey Dot." Darcy stepped down from his ladder to move it across to the next section. "We should be okay with the lights." He gave me a nod. "You could maybe start on the tinsel?"

There were stacks of boxes on one of the tables. Baubles and ornaments and piles of tinsel all mixed in together.

Uncle Ray strutted out of the office, lifting his hands like he was a director and we were his act. "Looking fantastic!" Then he came over to me. "I found all this at an op shop, can you believe it?"

I held up a faded, ceramic Santa with one eye worn away and a jagged end to his hat where a pom-pom used to be. "Oh, I believe it."

Uncle Ray sighed. "There'll be a lot of junk in here, but I'm sure we can salvage a few good bits. Go clock in first."

By the time I got back to the tinsel, Darcy and Flo were done with the lights, so they came around to help me.

A few times I caught Darcy mouthing words at me. It always took me a moment to realise he was only miming along to the music. I let myself grin and my cheeks turned warm as we tinseled our way around the restaurant, decorating the backs of chairs, the kitchen window frame and the corners of the walls.

It was a gold and silver scheme overall, because Flo said it would complement the fairy lights, and I'd trust Flo's judgment on anything aesthetic.

Darcy and I didn't talk too much. It was mostly Flo initiating the conversation, but I didn't mind. It was for the best. The more time I spent with him the more I thought about him. And I didn't want to let those thoughts consume me like they once had. Especially when they were unwarranted.

Seven o'clock came down upon us fast, and we rushed out back to get into our aprons while Uncle Ray himself seated the first table.

I felt like I was working in some angelic, magical haven with the fairy lights glinting gold against the wooden interior and sparkling tinsel. There was a possibility Uncle Ray had chosen today to put them up for that very reason. He knew it was my first shift back since the attack, and maybe he wanted to make it significant for other reasons. Better reasons.

I took the orders of a family of six with teen children. They were all warm and enthusiastic. The mother even told me the restaurant was looking *just beautiful*, and said that *Ray*–who she knew by name–should have the fairy lights up every night. A few customers seemed to have a rapport with Uncle Ray. Most would ask if he was in, and if he was, he would saunter out and sit with them for extensive lengths of time, chattering away.

If you knew Uncle Ray, you loved him–apart from his ex-wife, of course, but she was crazy so that didn't count.

I enjoyed the night. Darcy made it fun, though I hated to admit it. Our ebbing and flowing from the stand was almost therapeutic, and even though we didn't talk a whole lot, I started to relax in his company.

It was ten-thirty and only one table remained. Darcy and I wiped down all the others before finding ourselves without much left to do.

He sighed, folding his arms as I came to stand near him. "There's always one," he mused. "And they're usually middle-aged women."

"Well that's sexist," I said.

Darcy looked affronted. "It's true though!" He flapped a hand at the four ladies still speaking in murmurs. "You watch next time."

"Maybe we women just have more to say."

"No doubt," Darcy said, but he was grinning at me, and I got the feeling he was trying to stir me up. Then his expression faltered. "Speaking of which …"

I wet the cloth again and started wiping down the stand, even though it was already clean.

"What's been going on?" he asked, throwing me off enough that I looked right up at his beseeching eyes. "I haven't heard from you in like, two months. I've wondered—you been all right?"

"Oh." I looked away, rubbing the cloth over stubborn spots of dried fizzy drink splattered across the cupboards below the sink. "Yeah, I'm all right."

"You seem it now, but what happened in between?"

I gnawed at the inside of my cheek and considered whether I would be honest with my answer. Darcy was open and sincere, and that extended even to the cadence of his voice and the incline of his walnut-brown eyes. It was difficult to lie to a face like that.

"Well, I came back to Corner right after the attack, as you know ..." I stood and chucked the rag in the bin. Unsure what to do with my hands, I stretched out my fingers and held them tightly interlaced in front of me. "Then, I don't know. Things got worse. Your—Nina, she asked about that night when she came in."

Darcy blinked at me, then gave his head a shake. "Huh? When?"

"When she came into Corner to pick you up." I let that hang for a second or two, then ploughed right on. Maybe he wouldn't understand why I would care. "Anyway, it was around that time that I found it harder to leave the house, so I didn't. Not for ages. And then ..." Then Dad found Doctor Reem. Then I had therapy sessions in my living room, and then Flo and Emma pried me out of the black hole I'd been hiding in. He didn't need to know all the details. "A few people helped me see that I needed to get out again," I settled on. Truth in the vaguest sense of the word.

Darcy was frowning. "I'm glad, but—" he hesitated. "What did Nina say to you?"

I shrugged and attempted to appear unfazed by anything Nina could have said. "She basically just asked if they'd caught the guy who did it."

"Ah, shit," muttered Darcy. "She shouldn't have. It wasn't her place."

Why did you tell her at all? The bitter voice in my mind nearly forced itself between us. But I knew it was coming from a place of little reason, so I kept my mouth shut.

"I had to tell her," Darcy said, like he'd tracked my thoughts. "She asked why I got home so late that night and I couldn't really … lie."

"Mmm, of course." I nodded vigorously. Annoying as it was, he had a point. I couldn't have expected him to lie to his girlfriend. His loyalty was to Nina, not me. Whatever he owed me, it wasn't more than what he owed her.

"Wait." His frown burrowed deeper. "Is this why you weren't talking to me?"

"Pft." I forced a laugh but he didn't crack a smile, so I stopped pretty quickly. "Maybe."

Darcy sighed. "You should've said something."

"Do we pay here?" We both spun to find one of the ladies at the last table wielding her purse.

"Here is perfect," Darcy said, stepping up to take the payment. I sunk back into the kitchen, hoping to evade the conversation. Flo was there cleaning the coffee machine. I didn't mention anything about Darcy, even though a part of me wanted to sit down right there with cookies and milk and discuss it.

Instead I asked what she was doing tomorrow.

"I want to buy some new paints," she told me. "Metallic colours, just for something different. There's this little shop out in the Dandenongs I've always wanted to visit." She flicked me with the coffee rag. "Want to join?"

I tried not to look too happy about the fact that I now had a friend to hang out with on a Sunday. "Sure."

"What if I invited Jesse to come with us?" Now it was Flo's turn to play down her words. She was carefully folding the rag, even though it was dirty and needed to be thrown out anyway.

If I were Emma, I would've made a big hoo-ha out of the suggestion. But I wasn't Emma. I told Flo it was a lovely idea and maybe we could get lunch in Olinda too. Cameron once took me to a café there that baked fresh scones everyday, I added.

That's when Darcy came into the kitchen, a little red in the cheeks. "Want to learn how to clean the dishwasher?" he asked me.

"I'll leave you to it." Flo nudged my shoulder. "We'll text later about times." Then she breezed past us and turned the corner.

I was reminded of her painting—and how this was the very place she'd thought up the concept. Turning a corner. Stepping into an unknown. I'd found a home for it in my bedroom. Cluttered as my room was, there wasn't much on the walls. So I'd hung the canvas beside my cupboards, where I could see it from bed before I went to sleep.

Darcy bent to the dishwasher and turned to beckon me closer. "This is initiation," he said, once I was at his level. "Legend has it, once you've cleaned the dishwasher, you never leave Corner." He drew his voice into a whisper. "*Ever*. That's why Jesse's been here so long."

We were so close our knees were brushing and I was breathing the clean scent of his cologne.

"I don't know if I'm ready," I whispered back, with the same gravity he had.

"I think you are." Darcy pried open the dishwasher and proceeded to point out all the corners that tended to fill with grot. We took turns collecting fresh paper towels and bending low again to scrape out the muck. I almost gagged once.

"Isn't it a worry that this is the place dishes are supposed to *get* clean?" I posed with a shudder.

Darcy nodded, his nose crinkling and lips turning down at the corners. "You're not wrong."

The next step was to take a hose from the wall opposite to blast the remaining dirt. Darcy handed it to me and showed me where to direct the jet. I pointed the hose and squeezed the trigger–just as Darcy cried out, "*Wait!*" Water blasted my face.

I gasped. Spluttered. Let go.

There was only a short silence before Darcy exploded into laughter. I didn't move, just knelt there in shock, dripping from my nose and chin.

"I'm so–I'm sorry–" Darcy laid a hand on my back, trying to keep a straight face. When I looked up at him he was off again, his eyes crinkling shut.

I wasn't sure if I was halfway to tears or to laughter, but because of Darcy I tumbled into giggles.

It seemed a *serious* design flaw that the front of the hose should look identical to the back. My shoulders shook as I threw it away and tried to scramble to my feet.

"I'm just seeing it," he said, imitating a jet in the face with his hand, "over and over. Are you okay?" Again—a hand to my back. Even though his touch was unfamiliar, it didn't feel out of place. It felt careful and warm through my shirt.

The layers of reserve built up between us seemed to have fizzled in an instant. And because of that, I picked up the hose again and turned it on Darcy.

I squeezed the trigger.

An uncharacteristic, maniacal hoot rose from me as the water shot out. Darcy choked and threw his hands in front of his face as he lunged forward—then ducked to grab my legs. I was caught off guard. The kitchen tipped upside-down and I yelped in surprise.

Darcy swung me until the hose dropped from my grip and clattered to the ground.

When he set me down, we were both soaked. He was standing close enough that I could see every drop of water rolling down his cheeks and over the frame of his lips. I felt the sudden urge to lean forward and kiss them.

Darcy's gaze flickered to my mouth too. Was he thinking the same thing?

A rush of movement caught my eye over his shoulder. I caught the very end of a long ponytail disappearing back around the corner. Flo had come in—and left just as fast. I was fairly sure Darcy hadn't noticed, but it still drew me sharply out of the moment.

I gestured to the floor. "We made a mess."

Darcy nodded and backed away from me through the puddles, running a hand through his dark blonde hair, which was now soaked an oaky brown. "We can say the dishwasher exploded or something."

"Foolproof," I agreed.

To finish up, Darcy took the hose and cleaned out the dishwasher the way I was supposed to—not without pointing it menacingly back at me every now and then. We used almost an entire roll of paper towel to soak up the water.

When we made our way to the back office Flo had already gone. But Jude was there, tapping away on his computer. "What was all that yelling for?" he asked without turning.

Darcy laid his finger in the scanner to sign out, glancing back at me as if I had the answer. And he'd given it to me earlier, only it wasn't a sensible one.

I decided to say it anyway. "The dishwasher exploded."

Jude snapped to attention. "Did it really?"

"No," Darcy chimed, stepping aside so I could reach the scanner. "But it wouldn't be the worst thing. That one is on its last legs, surely. How long have we actually had it for?"

"Probably a century or so," Jude said with a sigh. "I'll talk to Ray about it. Hey–" He finally spun his chair around to face us. "Good to have you back, Dorothy."

"Thanks." I returned his smile. As we walked out from the office Jude called after us, "Either of you want to work tomorrow?"

"Uh, Mum has me running some errands!" Darcy called back. He looked at me and shook his head and I stifled a laugh.

"Dot?" Jude tried.

"I–I have plans too, sorry!"

"Useless," came the reply, as we continued on through the dim restaurant. Darcy pulled the door open for me.

"Thanks," I said.

"That's okay." The dark car park made my nerves start to jitter, but they were cut abruptly short as Darcy said–"Remember that time you walked straight into the glass?"

36

Even as I pulled up at home, I was still thinking about Darcy. After all this time, it had finally been revealed. He'd seen me that day. That fateful day I walked straight into a glass door and run off like a frightened, disorientated rabbit. I'd blocked it from my mind, but it was back to haunt me.

Darcy had chuckled all the way to our cars and I completely forgot to be nervous about the night or the car park. I forgot about a lot of things when I was with him—like how it hadn't been long since he and Nina had ended their relationship.

In fact, could I even be sure they had? Often couples seemed to spring back together after their first break-up attempt. Maybe she'd fought to get him back. I doubted any girl would feel sure of a decision to give up someone like Darcy.

If Jesse came to pick up Flo's paints tomorrow, maybe I could coax information out of him. Subtly, of course.

She texted shortly after I got into bed.

Flo: *Jesse's driving. Will pick you up 10ish x*

I had to resist the temptation to ask her if she'd seen Darcy and me in the kitchen. I'd raise it tomorrow if the chance arose.

I couldn't sleep that night, but not for the usual reasons. It was Darcy. Our water fight was on replay in my head. The way he'd so easily picked me up, and the marginal shift of his eyes to my lips. I was imagining what would've happened if I'd leant in—when I ordered myself to *stop*.

Zero expectations. Zero. If Darcy was interested in me, he would have to make it known. He was the one who'd just come out of a relationship, if the rumours were true. Until then, I wouldn't entertain the idea.

———◆———

I heard the car from my bedroom—hastily dancing myself into a pair of linen shorts and shoving my feet into a pair of white Converse.

"Going out with friends," I told Mum, who was rifling through a cardboard box in the lounge room.

"Oh." I sensed her snap to attention but I kept moving for the door. "Where to? Who's driving?"

"The Dandenongs—and I'm not driving."

"When will you be back?"

"I'm not sure, Mum." I knew it frightened her every time I left the house. But it couldn't always be that way. I had to learn how to do it, and she had to learn let me.

"I wanted your help with decorations today," she said, frowning at a tangle of fairy lights she pulled out of the box. "Less than three weeks till Christmas, can you believe? We haven't even done the tree."

"I'll do it when I get back." I gave her a quick air kiss before stepping outside. Jesse was parked in the driveway. Flo grinned from the passenger window as I approached.

"Hey." I dropped into the backseat. "Thanks for picking me up."

"No problem," Jesse said. "We have one more stop too. I invited Darc. Is that cool?"

I answered with a short and not at all excitable, "Sure."

Flo turned to me, a faint smile on her face. I hoped she hadn't proposed the idea to Jesse, or told him what I was feeling for Darcy. We started to drive and my phone vibrated in my pocket.

I pulled it out to see a text from Flo.

Flo: *Jesse suggested it. He doesn't know anything.*

Did she think something happened between me and Darcy? I guess it would've looked that way in the kitchen, considering how fast she bolted. I wished Jesse wasn't in the car. I wanted to tell Flo everything and pick it all apart together.

Darcy's house was only about fifteen minutes from mine. It was a street I'd driven past my whole life without ever going down. The houses were smaller than those in my area, but just as pictur-esque. Darcy's was an eggshell white weatherboard place with an iron fence and manicured garden.

"I know," Jesse said, and I realised he'd been watching me. "They even grow their own veggies. Apparently his Mum is obsessed with the garden."

"She'd get along well with my parents then," muttered Flo.

"Yeah ..." Jesse held a finger to his lips, then directed it at her. "They own their own business, right?"

Flo sighed. "Yup. Want to text Darc?"

Nodding, Jesse got out his phone and we heard the swish as his message went through. "So, what's it called?"

Flo frowned across at him. "What?"

"Your parents' business."

"Oh." Her mouth twisted. "*Morgan Bulbs.*"

Jesse glanced back at me, and I could see he was trying to hold a straight face.

"People don't get you confused with a light company?" I asked. Jesse let a snort slip, but I didn't really mean it as a joke.

"Funny you should say that," Flo said, "cos' it's actually happened a few times. But a lot of their business is word-of-mouth. So they don't seem too fussed."

"*Morgan Bulbs*," Jesse muttered under his breath, tapping the steering wheel. Just then, Darcy appeared at his front door. He was in denim shorts, those black Adidas runners and a black tee to match.

Behind him, something small and hairy burst from the door and shot out between his legs. He shouted after it. In a flash, the little dog was at the gate, ears high and tongue flopped out of its mouth as it fixated on the car.

I couldn't stop myself from smiling as Darcy scooped it up and raised a *one moment* finger at us.

"You can bring him!" Jesse called—before winding down Flo's window. "You can bring him if you want," he said again.

Darcy turned with an incredulous look. "Really?"

"The more the merrier."

Soon enough, there were five of us in the car. Darcy had ducked inside to get a leash and some other bits and bobs, but now we were all set to go.

The dog sat between us, bolt upright and watching the road ahead. I was more of a cat person, obviously, but I couldn't deny he was pretty cute.

"His name's Johnny," Darcy told me, smoothing his ears back. "Like, Johnny Bravo. I was really into that show when we got him, so please don't judge me. It was years ago."

"We're judging you," Jesse said from the front.

I couldn't judge him. My cat was *Kramer*, after all. And I'd also named every toy from my childhood after characters from The Saddle Club and 7th Heaven.

Jesse played classical music the entire drive up to the Dandenongs. I wouldn't have taken him for the classical type, but I quite liked it. "Let it wash over you," he said whimsically, in response to Flo's protests.

"I actually dig it," Darcy said, nodding along to a particularly hearty strings break. I smiled at him, like, *do you really?* And he laid his hand on his heart. "Genuinely."

Jesse turned up the volume and lowered all the windows so the wind whipped hair all over my face. I glanced across at Darcy, who was now vigorously playing an air violin. A laugh burst out of me, completely muffled by the music.

The art store was near Olinda, so we stopped there first. It was tucked amongst the trees at the end of a lengthy dirt driveway. Jesse kept the windows open just a crack for Johnny, and Flo just about sprinted for the shop.

Jesse turned to us at the door to whisper, "Someone's excited."

We dispersed when we got inside. Everything was cluttered and smelt like markers and dusty paper. I gravitated toward the painting paper, which was laid out beside blank sketchbooks and journals. I did need a new one. I was rifling through them when Darcy appeared beside me, holding one of those wooden figurines with bendy limbs.

"What would you think if you saw this in someone's room?" he said. "Like, seriously. Would you hang around?"

I grabbed it off him and laughed. "They help with sketching the correct proportions. We had them in the art room at school."

Darcy shook his head, frowning down at it as I bent the arm backwards. "Whose arm bends that way though?"

"I take your point," I conceded, passing it back to him. "Maybe you could write a letter telling them to factor inflexibility into their figurines."

"Maybe I will," he said, setting it onto the nearest shelf. "What you looking for?"

"Oh. Just a journal."

"Yeah? Nice. Do you keep a diary?" Curiosity lit up his eyes and the question didn't sound condescending because of it.

Still, I felt heat rush into my cheeks. "Sort of," I said. "I always loved to write, even back at school. Only, I didn't do it much just because. Not until … recently."

Darcy nodded. "What do you write about?" I must have looked a little taken aback, because he added, "You don't have to say," and bent to grab a block of watercolour paper. He started flicking through it as if there were something to see in the blank pages.

"I wrote about that night a couple of months back," I said, attempting to sound casual. "And how I've been feeling about it since." I didn't have to specify what night I was referring to. He knew.

"Oh, of course." Darcy picked up another sketch-book and cracked it open. "Am I in it?"

I blinked at him. "Huh?"

"From that night." He looked at me, his lips twitching. "Do I feature in the story?"

"Uh … sort of."

"I'm just being silly," he said, shutting the book and setting it down. "I still feel bad about Nina bringing it up with you."

On the outside, I batted the comment away. Inside–I went tense. "She probably meant well."

"You'd be surprised," he muttered. "But that's over, anyway."

"Oh, really?"

Darcy nodded, then shrugged. "Yeah. It's a long story, but–she was really demanding. To the point of … yeah. Anyway. It's good now." Darcy talked a lot without saying much.

"I'm sorry to hear." Was that the right thing to say to a boy you liked who'd just broken up with a girl you didn't like?

"Nah, nah. It's all cool."

There was a hiss behind us. We spun to see Jesse's face peering through the shelves of grey leads. "I think we lost Flo," he said.

We moved around the shop until we found a side avenue filled with acrylic paints. Flo was at the very end of it, tubes just about tumbling out of her hands and multiple brushes tucked behind her ear.

"That's awesome," Jesse said, and I turned to see him smirking at her. "A glimpse into her natural habitat."

I wondered what would be considered my natural habitat. It was a rare place where I felt natural in every sense of the word. Maybe it was sitting on my bed with Kramer on my lap and a book in my hand. It wasn't an impressive picture, but it was a comfortable one.

Did natural habitat refer to the place you existed most, or the place you were mostly yourself? Maybe the aim of life was to make a natural habitat of every place you went–to be your truest self through the unfamiliar as well as the familiar. What if I was just as comfortable outside the house as I was inside my room with Kramer for company? How different would things look?

37

I lay on my back with thick grass tickling my cheeks. Flo's head rested against me, and Jesse and Darcy sat either side of us. We'd had a bite to eat in Olinda and driven down to the Alfred Nicholas Memorial Gardens. Jesse knew where to go, because he'd been there before to take photos—and it was certainly worthy of it. Small patches of grass accessible by sturdy wooden bridges cut into a lake speckled with green leaves.

I'd picked a small, purple flower on our way down to keep as a reminder of the day. It would fit nicely on my memento shelf.

We were set up by the water, with Johnny pacing only so far as his lead would take him while Jesse told us more about the course he was applying for at RMIT.

"You get to do an internship too, as part of it," he explained. "So that would be pretty sweet."

I heard a click, and then Flo said, "Hey!" Quickly lifting my head, I saw Jesse grinning behind a small camera.

"Delete it," Flo demanded.

His expression turned earnest. "I don't know how to."

"*Jesse*."

"*Flo*–it's film. You can't just delete film."

She groaned, and then tilted her head back to cast me a dubious glare. "Convenient," she murmured.

"We should do this more often," Darcy said. I turned to face him, just as he slid to the grass beside me. "Make a tradition of it." He squinted into the sun, and then turned his squinty eyes my way, a smile teetering at the corner of his lips. I closed my eyes to shut him out.

He wasn't with Nina. I knew it for certain now. But that shouldn't mean I was next in line. I didn't want him to think I was waiting right there behind her.

"Those scones were delicious," Jesse said. "I'd come back just for them." We had all got the scones, and nobody was disappointed.

Flo picked at the grass and said, "Em will freak if she hears we did this without her."

Jesse snorted. "Who cares? It's not like her and Reese don't do things without us."

"That's true," granted Flo. "They do see each other a lot."

A hairy face loomed over me, followed by a wet tongue to the nose. I'd almost forgotten Johnny was here. I huffed and covered my face. When I lowered my hands, Darcy was watching me, smiling.

"He likes you," he said. "I can tell."

If only it were that easy.

———•———

Frank Sinatra sang to us that night after dinner—or at least he tried to, beneath Dad's determined attempts to override him. It was our Christmas tradition. We would take a night in December for me to decorate the tree, Mum to string up fairy lights and Dad to cook up my favourite potato bake and lamb roast.

I always thought it would be interesting to see how things would've turned out if my parents' roles had been reversed. If Dad had stayed at home and Mum had kept working at the pharmacy.

She hated cooking and Dad loved it. She was always prompt, whereas Dad always left late for work and preferred spontaneity over regimented order. He was the person to surprise you with an ice cream from the milk bar that he'd decided to pick up last minute on his way home, usually some weird flavour like macadamia nut and cranberry. Mum was the type to stock our fridge with at least ten classic Sara Lee cheesecakes, so she didn't have to even think about dessert for months after.

The smell of baked potatoes wafted from the kitchen where Dad was garnishing the lamb and whistling along to *The First Noel*. I was inspecting our collection of baubles, deciding whether to feature the ones I made in primary school from paper maché.

"Feels like yesterday, don't you think?" Dad said. "Last Christmas."

I considered. In some ways, it did. But it also felt as though it had taken place in some alternate dimension–one where the uni experience was still fresh and new, and Cameron was here to help me set up the tree, tying tinsel around my head like a bandana, when I didn't have a job and hadn't intersected with anyone at Corner. So much had changed between then and now.

I tied a paper maché bauble to the tree and finally answered, "Not to me."

38

The air conditioner in Doctor Reem's office was struggling. It was *hot*, and not pleasant summer hot either, but dry, baking heat typical of Melbourne in December.

Doctor Reem was asking me about my journal. I told her honestly that I was writing less about the attack and more about my friends. *Mostly Darcy*– but I left that detail out.

"How are you feeling now about it all?" she said, narrowing her owl eyes at me in that contemplative way.

"Better." I traced a flower on the armrest of my couch. Doctor Reem had decked out her office in furniture you might find in your grandparents house, but I liked that about it. There were pressed petals and leaves in frames on the walls and an antique desk behind her. It felt unintimidating. Homey. Maybe I could press and frame the flower I took from the gardens in the Dandenongs. It would last longer that way–the flower and the memory.

"Night is worse than daytime," I told her. "But to be honest, I've always been anxious. Even before the attack. So I don't know if I'm still panicked from that time or if I'm back to my *normal* self."

She nodded slowly. "Have you heard of social anxiety?"

Uh-oh. That sounded scarily accurate.

"It's more common than you think," Doctor Reem went on, adjusting her glasses. "Many people experience mild forms of it." She went on to describe the symptoms–sweating, increased heart rate, blushing, shaking, difficulty looking people in the eye. I admitted to experiencing almost all of them, and added my lip gnawing to the list.

Doctor Reem asked me for examples of times I'd felt this way. So I mentioned Reese's party and how I'd sat in my car for ages before convincing myself to go home, and how I often worried about what I said before I said it, and that I hated being the centre of attention.

I was starting to think Doctor Reem had magical powers, because somehow I wound up telling her what I'd never told anyone else. That I felt small, insignificant and silly–too often. I told her that I hated the name Dot, but I hated Dorothy more. It all came out like a woeful stream and by the end I realised Doctor Reem had barely uttered two words.

She set down her notepad and looked out the window. And then, very calmly, she told me I wasn't small, or insignificant, or silly. She said that the voice convincing me of these things was lying and that I would learn to drown it out.

Doctor Reem ran me through a few techniques: slow breathing, taking walks, voicing the anxious feelings with people I trusted, and setting goals for myself–even as simple as looking a stranger in the eye with intention. She said my work at Corner would allow me a space to practice.

I felt some relief when she told me that being alone could be positive too, a time to recharge and collect my thoughts. It was about balance and that would look different for everybody. But *nobody* should feel they had no choice but to leave a party before it began.

At my car, I paused for a moment and turned my face up to the sun. It was too hot, but I let myself feel it.

Voicing my fears had unlocked a door inside me that was previously bolted shut. A door I'd never even seen before. My shyness was partially just who I was. But the sweaty-palmed, racing-hearted anxiety that accompanied it wasn't.

Because when I felt most me, my palms were dry and my heart was steady.

39

It was all over the news. Her name was Riley Matthews. She had been walking through a park in the city after meeting two friends at a bar. The police didn't know if the attack was opportunistic or premeditated. They hadn't caught anyone yet.

She had called her boyfriend shortly before it had happened, to tell him she was safe. She was on her way home. She wouldn't be long.

There were signs of assault, but no further details on that were released. They suspected her body had been left for two hours, before the jogger found it.

I thought a lot about that jogger. What must have gone through his mind, when he first saw her there? How long did it take him to believe it?

The night I first heard the story, I couldn't sleep. I dreamed that it was my body. My family left to deal with it. My loss. Their loss.

It could have been worse. What happened to me could've been worse. But I wasn't telling myself that as a self-indulgent comfort. The words felt more like a self-inflicted accusation.

It could have been worse.

She was killed. *You weren't.* She wasn't here to talk about it, or to go for ice cream or put up her Christmas tree. *You are.*

When you thought the worst had happened to you, you could be sure that it hadn't.

The next morning I lay in bed a while staring out the window. I could see the tops of Mum's maple trees swaying in the wind under a sliver of blue sky.

I thought of Riley Matthews and how unfair it was that she wasn't waking up today. That she wouldn't see the trees or the sky ever again.

It could have been worse. But it wasn't. I was still here. Breathing. It was terrifying and unjust that the decisions of strangers had the power to bind our lives and even end them.

Two birds cut an arc through the blue, ducking below my window frame. Somehow, this was the moment I realised that living wasn't a solo act. We had to live for the people that weren't walking, talking, laughing or running anymore.

Jesse had to go on because his sister couldn't. I had to get up because Riley wouldn't.

40

I approached Corner with a spring in my step—a plan to put Doctor Reem's suggestions into practice with customers and even with Darcy. I'd say what I wanted to say and try not to think it over three times before gathering the courage. I'd look people in the eye, long enough to squirm and then a little longer. I'd walk with a straight back. They were small steps, but I was excited to try them all out. The new Dot, just a little bigger than the speck she had been before.

Riley Matthews was still on my mind, and maybe my enthusiasm to change had something to do with her too. A defiant act in the face of her killer and my attacker. Both still faceless. Proving to myself and to them that if one falls, the other can get stronger, not stop too.

I knew I couldn't click my fingers and shed all my layers. But I could pretend. And then, just maybe, they would eventually fall away.

I passed Darcy at the stand, looked him straight in the eye with a smile and said, "Hi."

"Hey," he said back, and before I carried on I caught the waver of a frown, as if he'd noticed the difference.

My heart was racing as I went out the back to sign in. Okay, so I could direct my eye line easily enough, but my heart wasn't so easy. I wasn't a wizard. Geez. That part would have to follow.

On my first trip to the kitchen I found Flo making coffees. We had a lot to catch up on. I hadn't even clarified what happened or didn't happen between me and Darcy that day she'd seen us in the kitchen.

So, acting on the instinct I usually preferred to stifle, I went up to her and said that we had things to discuss. The bemused smile and low nod of assent she gave me settled my nerves well enough.

A bit later into the night, Darcy was entering an order into the screen at the stand when I came up behind him to do the same. He cast me a side-eye and I saw the corner of his cheek lift a little. "I was thinking kebabs after work," he said without turning, "if you're down."

I noticed then that he seemed slightly nervous, which made my efforts to stay calm a little easier. Sometimes I felt like there was an anxiety metre between two people at any given time. If somebody was halfway nervous, you took up the other half. If they were a little nervous, you were the rest. Maybe that's why I was always so uneasy. If I felt like the other person wasn't at all, I used up the whole metre for the both of us.

"Or we could go somewhere else." Darcy shrugged and busied himself with tucking his note-pad in the front of his apron. "Doesn't have to be kebabs. Or, if you're busy we don't have to–"

"Sure," I said, and I looked him in the eye while I smiled. One second. Two. Three. He was the first to break. I thought I even saw his cheeks flush. Wow. The power of eyes. If only I'd known sooner.

I practically pranced up to the next table. Judging by the startled expressions of the two ladies at the receiving end of my, "Hello there", I might have over-cooked my cheeriness. But I couldn't help it. One joyous word was on an endless turn in my mind.

Kebabs.

Kebabs.

Kebabs.

Was it just me involved in this plan? Was it an *I want to spend time with you* kebabs or a *let's get a group together* kebabs? Either way it had me glid-ing through the restaurant all night. Not just because of Darcy, but because I felt different. Like there was less separating me from the world.

There was goodness to see and I was starting to see it when I looked people in the eye and made the effort to smile without restraint. When I spoke a few words to the chef between taking meals. When I tapped Darcy's shoulder only to duck to the opposite side and watch him turn the wrong way. You missed a lot when you were too scared to look.

———◆———

By the end of the shift, *kebabs* were still an ambiguous invitation. While I was packing the last of the dirty dishes into the dishwasher, Flo poked me and hissed, "What's going on with you and Darc?"

I flicked a few soggy chips into the bin from the last plate. Darcy's music was loud over the restaurant speakers, so I figured he couldn't hear us. "What do you mean?"

Flo drew her voice even lower and her blue eyes turned sparkly. "The other night, in here." She pointed at the floor, as if what happened the other night could be seen on the tiles if we looked hard enough. "Are you going to tell me what happened?"

"Nothing!" I couldn't wipe my smile, even though I knew it didn't help my case. "Promise," I added to strengthen it. "But, he did ask if I wanted to grab food after work."

"Oh?" Flo raised her brows with all the insinuation her tone conveyed. She went to the bin and started digging through it.

I stepped aside so she could get closer. "What are you looking for?"

"My invite," she said. "Must be in here somewhere …"

I knocked her elbow and left the kitchen, still grinning. It was then that I noted Darcy's absence.

Bins? No. They were still full.

My gaze caught on two figures by the window outside. One was Darcy, his arms folded across his apron. The other was Nina.

Why was she here? They were broken up. Darcy said it himself. He told me in the art shop and that wasn't long ago. Had things changed since then?

And if they had, why was he inviting me to get kebabs? Maybe it really didn't mean anything.

Darcy had already wiped the tables, so I started tilting chairs, my eyes skimming the window as often as they could without being obvious. Nina was walking away, into the car park. My heart sunk as Darcy ducked his head and jogged after her.

I swallowed the lump in my throat. It wasn't a big deal. It didn't matter. We weren't anything anyway.

But she really shouldn't have been here because Darcy was working. He wasn't getting paid to speak to Nina. And it was a dog move to make me close up the restaurant alone. Where were they even going?

Flo popped out of the kitchen, rolling her apron over her arm. "Where's Darcy?" She came closer, a smirk forming. "Getting ready for your kebabs date?"

I couldn't even feign a smile. "Nina's here."

"What?" Flo was at the window before I could even gesture to it. "What the hell? What are they doing?"

I shrugged and started checking salt and peppershakers. If I looked outside, my heart might just fall right through me.

"Okay … they're hugging," Flo commentated, causing my teeth to grit together. "They're actually hugging. What is going on? I thought–" She didn't finish the sentence, but she didn't have to. I thought too. Or at least, I hoped.

"It's all good," I said dismissively, while I kicked myself for building up *kebabs* to be anything at all. And I definitely shouldn't have told Flo about it. Now I felt extraordinarily pathetic.

"I was going to leave you to it, but …" Flo turned back to me and hesitated. "Want me to hang around?"

"Maybe." I wanted to get out of there. Fast.

"You finish the tables," said Flo. "I'll do the bins."

"No it's all right, bins are the worst–"

"Say no more," she interjected, making for the stand.

We were done in five minutes, and Darcy still wasn't back. So we said goodbye to Jude and signed out.

It was only as we were walking back through Corner that Darcy appeared again. His cheeks were red and he was breathing hard.

"Hey," he said. "Sorry, I was just … I'm back. What's left to do?"

"Nothing," Flo answered for me.

I felt my lips pull tight and I tried to smile. But my *pretending I'm okay* smile was about as convincing as my photo face.

"Oh." Darcy whipped toward me. "You still—okay no worries. You heading off?"

"Yeah," I said, following Flo to the door. Part of me wanted to suggest kebabs. The other part wanted to go home and climb into bed and not think at all about Darcy or Nina or anything to do with kebabs.

I felt Darcy's eyes on us as we left, but I didn't look back at him.

DARCY

She was supposed to arrive at Corner *before* my shift started. But typically, Nina came when she wanted to. I swear sometimes she just did it to make a point. But three years into the relationship—I still had no idea what that point was.

I was bent over the table nearest the door when I saw her strutting up the steps toward the restaurant. The last time Nina met Dot, she'd brought up the attack. I couldn't risk that happening again, so I dropped my rag and ran outside.

Nina stopped short. The first thing I noticed was that she'd done her makeup the way she normally did before going out, which included those fake lashes that were so thick and heavy I swear they made her eyes narrower. Also she was wearing that woollen-collared denim jacket she knew I liked. Why? Was she really trying to impress me now? Seemed kinda pointless.

"Stuff's in my car," she said. "Want to come grab it?"

I just said, "Hello," mostly to point out that she hadn't. But Nina wasn't here to play nice–I could see it in the hard set of her jaw.

Over all the years I'd known her, I'd come to realise that Nina was an angel to her friends and practically the devil to her enemies. If you received the first version, you couldn't help but adore her the way I had. You saw her attention as a privilege, because she was selective in who she chose to feature in her life and if you found yourself in it–*lucky you*.

We'd got together at the end of high school, and back then the line between her friends and enemies was more distinct. It seemed that the less clear it became, the more our problems grew. For example–it wasn't funny anymore when Nina treated people like shit. I couldn't laugh it off. Especially when it was me being treated that way.

She folded her arms and peered into Corner. "Who's working tonight?"

"Flo and Dot," I said shortly.

"Huh." Nina looked back to me, pointedly. She hated Corner. Despised it, actually, and not only for the fact that I was working with other girls. What had come out through many long, heated discussions over the last few months was that she viewed my shifts as a prioritizing of work over our relationship. Just the way she saw my soccer games and training.

The guys on the team had been on my case about it for so long that I'd stopped bringing her up around them.

You don't set aside enough time for me. You don't put in enough effort. So I suppose the errands I ran almost daily for Nina *and* her parents counted for nothing. And the fact that I would visit her place ten times more than she would mine, and organise city date nights each month, and bring her ice cream whenever she was feeling down.

That was what did it, in the end. Realising that I could never do enough–*be* enough for her. Because her expectations sky-rocketed above my head, and the expectations I had of her, like *being a nice person*–she couldn't seem to meet either.

Nina spun on her heel and marched off toward her car. I hated when she did that, as if I was some puppy that would trail along behind her. It was the perfect metaphor for our whole relationship. I jogged to catch up and matched my pace with hers.

"Once I leave here I don't want you contacting me," she snapped, staring ahead. Ah, the melodrama. I wouldn't miss that.

"Okay," I said, and I knew it would piss her off a bit. She got a kick out of emotional reactions, but I didn't owe her anything now.

She jerked her car door open and heaved the amp out of the back seat. I had kept it at her place to practice bass because Mum claimed the vibrations gave her a headache.

My guitar came next, and I winced as she set it on the asphalt so hard I heard it knock against the lid.

"That's it then," she said crisply, as if our relationship could be tied off in three neat little words.

"You really want to leave it like this?" I took my guitar and laid it against the amp, turning back to face her. "After three years? *That's it then*?"

Nina's jaw was rock hard, her eyes fierce. The closest to sadness she ever got was rage. Once we went to see *The Fault in Our Stars* and she left the cinema absolutely furious with the ending. She wouldn't talk to me the entire way home.

When her pet rabbit Tony died I took over roses and a soft bunny toy, which she exploded about because apparently I was trying to replace Tony. *How dare I!*

"Well is there anything left to say?" Nina tilted her chin up. Savage. "I think we've done it all to death."

She wasn't wrong. We'd done it beyond death, followed it into the afterlife and beaten everything there to a pulp too.

"Kinda," I conceded. But it was weird–cutting a tie to someone you'd been bound to for so long. Despite all the shit I'd taken from her, it made me feel sick inside. And I knew that regardless of what she wanted, I couldn't have three years of my life ending like this.

So I stepped forward and wrapped my arms around her. Nina was stiff as a plank, at first. Then she softened just enough to lift her arms around me too.

"I want you to be happy," I told her, honestly.

"I am happy," came the stubborn, muffled response. I rolled my eyes over her head. Defiance till the end. How fitting.

———◆———

Dot was heading for the door behind Flo by the time I made it back to Corner. Shit. How much of the close had I missed?

"Hey. Sorry, I was just … I'm back. What's left to do?" I didn't know why I couldn't say I'd been meeting Nina. Maybe I didn't want Dot to know it. But surely it looked worse if I didn't have an excuse at all.

"Nothing," Flo said, and I sensed the dismissive note in her voice.

"Oh." I frowned. They were leaving? Dot cast me this small smile but quickly averted her eyes. She'd seemed different at the start of the shift. Now she was different again.

I could never quite figure her out. The very moment we'd met I'd wondered what she was all about. I'd tried to ignore the curiosity–until recently. Until Nina was no longer a factor.

Tonight, it hadn't felt so wrong to ask her if she was keen for kebabs. Why should it? She was funny and interesting and I enjoyed her company. I'd be lying if I said I didn't think she was exceptionally pretty too–but with an ex-girlfriend of all but a week, I couldn't let myself dwell on that. Not right now, anyway.

"You still–okay no worries." I scratched at my head. "You heading off?"

Dot said, "Yeah," without really looking at me. She struck me as someone who felt safer behind barriers–barriers she built from halfway smiles and nervous gestures. I'd had glimpses of what lay behind them, but never for long. They were back, and for some reason, it stung me to see it.

I made my way to the fingerprint scanner to clock off. The door to the office was open and Jude was inside, resting his chin in his palm while he clicked over rosters on the computer. Without looking away he said, "Where'd you go?"

"Huh?"

"You left for half your close. I saw on the cameras."

I shoved my finger into the scanner, waiting for the green light. "You watch the cameras? That's just–wow. Stalker."

Jude turned then, but I wheeled around and ducked down to the lockers. "Seriously, where were you?" he asked again.

I couldn't leave without relenting a bit. Jude liked to be *in the know* about absolutely everything, so if anyone dared to hide the truth around him, he would sniff it out like a freaking hound. "Nina," I said, swinging the strap over my shoulder. "She was returning some of my things."

Jude raised a brow. "On our time?"

"Yeah, sorry. She wasn't meant to—you can take it out of my pay."

"Calm down, Darcy, it's fine." Jude rolled his eyes. "What's going on? Is this a break up?"

"Kinda, yeah." It still felt weird to admit out loud.

"Wow." Jude's chair squeaked as he sunk back into it. "Why? Haven't you been dating for years?"

I nodded, and then gave a resigned shrug. "Shit happens, I guess."

"Dot?"

I frowned at him. "What Dot?"

Jude's face twisted. He was trying not to smile, I could tell. "Did it have anything to do with Dorothy?"

"Uh, no." I flicked my hair out of my eyes. "Of course not."

"Oh, okay," Jude said, with that same bemused glint in his eye. "You've just seemed a lot closer recently, from what I've seen."

"This dude–" I pointed at him, ignoring the sudden tension in my gut, "sits in his office all night and thinks he's seen it all." My laugh sounded forced, but I kept it up anyway.

Jude went back to his computer. "Just saying," he said. "I can sense these things, you know."

"Can you just–okay. Whatever." I cast him a wave and spun out into the restaurant.

At the door, I thought back to the day I met Dot, how she'd walked right into the glass. I could still see her holding her nose while she hurried away. I had almost run after her to check if she was all right, but I got the impression that the greater kindness would be to let her go.

Although Jude could be a sticky-beak pain in the arse–he was mostly right about things. Was he right about me and Dot?

42

Without the cards I'd thrown away, my collection could fit into one single folder. It seemed much more sensible, if keeping a business-card stash could be deemed sensible at all.

Once I had the folder positioned at the edge of my desk, my eyes rose higher to the shelf above it. The pepper grinder. It was nestled amongst all the other knick-knacks I'd kept over the years. I was tempted to chuck it, but I couldn't bring myself to do it. So instead, I shifted it to the back of the shelf, along with the purple flower from the Alfred Nicholas Memorial Gardens.

There were other things I could throw out. I'd forgotten the meaning behind a few, like some old ribbon fraying at the edges, a creepy fairy figurine, a dried rose so old it was literally dissolving. I tossed it all, and it felt good.

—•—

I was in bed, sniffling my way through JoJo Moyes' *Me Before You*—at Mum's recommendation—when a text came through from Lauren Price.

Lauren: *Hey lovely. Heard what happened to you. Omg. No words. Let me know if there's anything I can do xx*

Jenny would have told her a while ago, after meeting with Mum, but maybe Lauren had just heard about Riley Matthews and felt compelled to reach out because of that.

I put my phone down without answering. It was nice when someone thought of you, but a lot nicer when they thought of you when things were good too, not just when you'd been accosted with a knife.

I'd known Lauren most of my life, but I didn't want to talk to her about it. If anyone, I would go to Flo, or Jesse. Even Darcy, despite everything. I would go to the people I'd met only a few months ago. Sometimes it was timing that dictated the strength of a friendship, not time.

It was Uncle Ray's idea to have Christmas lunch at Corner. The restaurant was shut, so we'd have it all to ourselves. We were bringing a turkey, roast veggies and a sticky date pudding. Uncle Ray and Peter were on drinks and nibbles.

When we turned into the car park, I was sure our minds all went to the same place. But neither Mum nor Dad said anything.

I took the dessert dish and climbed out of the car. On our way over, I paused and turned back. "It was just over there," I said. "The third row down." Mum and Dad stopped in their tracks.

Why had Darcy checked my car that night at all? Had he seen me sitting in the backseat and wondered why I was there? Had he seen me on the ground and watched me clamber inside? He did ask if I'd fallen …

It didn't matter, anyway. We hadn't spoken properly since Nina visited Corner.

"Maybe coming here was a bad idea," murmured Mum.

"It's *okay*." I rolled my eyes at her. "I've been back since."

"But on Christmas …"

"All the more reason!" Dad interjected, and I felt his hand come to rest on my shoulder. "We spit in the face of adversity, don't we Dotty?"

"Yes, Dad." I cast him a smile and turned back to the restaurant.

Inside, Uncle Ray was behind the bar in a Santa hat, a black shirt and a red bow tie. Peter was wearing a red velvet suit, laying napkins on two tables they'd joined together in the centre of the main floor. The fairy lights were turned on, shining brightly above it.

A bunch of hugs and loud *Merry Christmas*'s went around before we settled into our places. I sat opposite Peter, with Mum and Dad beside us and Uncle Ray at the table's head. He went around filling our glasses with champagne.

I cast my gaze around the restaurant, letting it fall in the places that held the clearest memories.

The stand, where Darcy and I chattered in bursts throughout the night. The floor outside the kitchen where I once dropped a glass–Jesse had been there in seconds to sweep it up. Behind that kitchen window, Flo had taught me to make a fairly decent barista-style coffee. And that "*corner!*" into the kitchen, where I had strode back and forth announcing myself until it didn't feel embarrassing to yell anymore.

Despite the worst event of my life occurring outside of it, I loved this place. Because it was where the very best had happened, too.

"Raise your glasses." Uncle Ray stood and flicked the pom-pom on his Santa hat out of his face. "Today we are not only celebrating the birth of a baby, but the birth of a new chapter for us all."

"Here we go," Peter muttered, taking a swig of his champagne.

"Not yet!" Uncle Ray laid his hand flat across the rim of Peter's glass. "This is a chapter of love, promise, acceptance and success. If you're ready for it, join me *now* in a toast."

Mum and Dad raised their glasses, Peter pried Uncle Ray's hand away before lifting his too, and then I joined.

"To the next chapter," Dad declared, and we all drank.

———◆———

Peter and I sat on the steps to Corner, sipping from our champagne flutes. It was only my second drink for the night but I already felt it. I told Peter and he snorted.

"You're as bad as Dad," he said. "Two drinks in and he calls it quits."

"That's because his personality is already two drinks in, so he's basically on four."

"Fair point," Peter conceded. He pulled out a cigarette and lit up. I didn't often accompany him when he smoked, but it was Christmas and Mum, Dad and Uncle Ray were still inside.

"So Dad's gay." Peter's words clanged against the silence. As they sunk in, I turned slowly to face him.

"*What?*"

"Yep." He slid a tight-lipped smile my way between drags. "Told me this morning. He's dating that manager dude."

I stared at him, wide-eyed. "I can't tell if you're being serious." But even as I said it, I knew he was. When Peter made a joke, he'd laugh before you did. Neither one of us was laughing now. "Jude?"

"That's the one." Peter sipped at his champagne.

"Why are you not more shocked about this?" I demanded.

"Oh, I've known for ages."

I just continued to stare at him, until he looked at me and rolled his eyes. "His trips to Sydney every second weekend? Please. I knew something was up. Why make the effort to travel that often if you could check in with the Corner branches over the phone?"

"He doesn't go to Sydney?"

"He goes occasionally, not every time. One night like a year ago, I tracked his phone signal. Turned out he was just a couple of suburbs over." Peter sucked on his cigarette and I was tempted to pluck it out of his mouth and throw it so he could hurry up and finish the story. But I tapped my foot on the step and waited. "So I sussed out the address. Waited a while and finally saw Dad through the window drinking wine on the couch, with that Jude guy."

"Oh boy."

Peter wiggled his eyebrows at me. "Oh boy indeed."

"But did you tell him you knew already?" I asked, still bewildered.

"Nah, didn't want to embarrass the old man. I knew he'd get around to telling me, if it was anything serious."

"And it's serious?"

"It's serious."

"Geez." I set my champagne down beside me and hugged my knees. "Who would've thought?"

"He's always been a bit … out there. *Eccentric*, some might say."

"I guess." Uncle Ray was many things. He was kind and brash and thoughtful and generous. But the thing he was most of all, he had kept entirely to himself. And for so long. I'd never thought to read into the fact that he never seriously dated anyone else after Aunty Rhea. But now, it made sense.

Had he not told us because he thought we'd react badly? Remembering Mum and Dad, I peered back around into the restaurant. Uncle Ray was leaning across the table, speaking rapidly to them with this strained look on his face and his hands working double-time to match the pace of his words. "Wait … he's not–"

"Telling them? Yep, I think he is."

I snapped around to Peter. Dad would be chill about it, but I wasn't so sure about Mum. I didn't want to watch her finding out.

"Well." I set my hands on the pavement behind me and leaned back into them. "There you go."

I cast my eyes above the car park to the sky. It was a clear night and the stars were on show. Maybe you didn't always have to drive a long way to see them. I caught myself wondering whether Darcy had noticed.

"You know, he thinks you're killing it here," Peter said, letting a stream of smoke slip from his lips and nose.

I turned my hazy gaze on him. "Uncle Ray?"

"Yep. All the dubs sing your praises, apparently."

I smiled and wondered who exactly had sung.

"And I think he's impressed you came back after everything that happened." Peter paused, and then slanted his gaze to me. "Don't tell him I told you this, but he's been going on about giving you a management position."

"*What?* You can't be serious. I just started!"

"Not now, doofus." Peter chuckled and shook his head. "In the future. I'm not interested in inheriting the business, as you know, so I guess he's setting his sights on the next best thing."

The next best thing. Peter was such an arse. But then, in his mind it was probably the biggest compliment he could bestow.

And maybe it wasn't so farfetched. I *was* studying Business Management, after all. If my end goal wasn't to manage a business, what the heck was I doing?

"I think he's got the wrong person," I said anyway.

Peter shrugged. "That's what I keep telling him."

"Oi." I shoved his knee.

"Hey, hey! The suit!" He lifted his champagne and cigarette high and raked his eyes over the sleeves. Trust Peter to buy a red velvet suit. He looked like a young Hugh Hefner.

"Is your New Year's resolution going to be to quit smoking?" I asked, because I knew it always was and I knew he never could.

He narrowed his eyes at me and dragged on the cigarette, then blew the smoke into my face. I spluttered and flapped my hands to disperse it.

"Actually it's to accept defeat," he said. "What's yours? Try not to get mugged again?"

I might have snapped back, but I was the one who started the digs so I resisted. "Actually, it's to go more places I've never been before."

Peter got to his feet and turned, resting one foot on a higher step. "Lame."

"You're such a dickhead."

"Give me more!" he said, spreading his arms with almost as much flourish as Uncle Ray might. "My Dad's coming out of the bloody *closet* and you're just going to drive a few new places? What are you gonna *achieve* Dorothy the Dinosaur?"

He would never understand that going new places *was* an achievement. At least for me. So I decided to stir him up instead.

"I'm going to become the best damn waitress the world has ever seen."

"God help us all." Peter shook his head and I just grinned back.

44

When Peter and I went inside, all three heads at the table turned toward us. Mum's shoulders were sitting up high and her face was pale even though she was smiling. Dad was bright red, and Uncle Ray looked caught somewhere between discomfort and relief.

"Dotty," he said, a little too briskly. "I suppose now is as good of a time as any—"

"I already told her," Peter cut in.

Uncle Ray's brows rose high. "You did?"

"Yep." Peter drained the last of his champagne. "Is there any more of this?" When nobody answered, he shrugged and moved off to the bar.

I didn't know what to say. None of us did, it seemed. So I went with, "It's all right, Uncle Ray," and then realised how pitiful it sounded. I wasn't trying to comfort him. I just wanted to convey that I was glad he felt able to share himself in full. Even if it had taken this long. That everything was *all right*. That nothing had changed between us.

Dad jumped on my bandwagon. "Course it's all right," he said, while his ears glowed bright red.

"We're family. We support each other through anything. Right Kat?"

Mum's face was pinched, but she nodded. "Right."

"Just don't go hitting on me anytime soon," Dad said, before letting out a staggered laugh. I poured myself a glass of water to hide my cringe. There were sure to be a few clangers while we all adjusted to the revelation–mostly from my father. Maybe I *could* understand why Uncle Ray kept it from us all this time.

"I think we need to toast again," Dad said, his voice still too loud. "Let's toast! Come on. Peter! Where are you?"

Peter sauntered over with a full glass in one hand and a bottle in the other.

"What did you say before, Ray? To a new chapter?" Dad was blustery and nervous now, but it was so adorable and ridiculous that I found myself falling into a fit of uncontrollable giggles. To my surprise, Mum joined me. And that set off Uncle Ray too.

"What's so funny?" Dad looked between us all. "I'm trying to do a nice thing!"

"I know, Jim." Mum patted his arm. "I know." She gave me a look and held her glass to the level of Dad's. "To a new chapter," she said. "And all the chapters after."

45

"Remind me again why I'm doing this?" Flo whispered over her shoulder while I tugged her hair into a loose plait.

"Because you're a smitten kitten—now face forward," I said, smiling.

"I feel ridiculous." Flo sighed, and then she called out, "I don't want to be in every one!"

Jesse was standing at the cliff's edge peering through his camera lens. The wind whipped his hair in every direction. He looked wild and serene at the same time, and I thought then that someone ought to take a photo of *him*.

"Relax," he said, sauntering back toward us with his eyes glued on the camera screen. "This time it's digital. Deletable."

"Are you implying my face is deletable?" Flo inquired, and I stifled a giggle while Jesse rolled his eyes.

"I can never win," he said. But he had. They'd been dating for a month or so now, and in my opinion, he couldn't have won anything better.

Flo's hair was done, and when she rose to standing, she looked like a regal elf. Jesse had her in this flowing white dress that fell just above her bare toes and a transparent, orange scarf that draped over her shoulders and highlighted the flecks of orange in the rocky outcrop around us. "Galadriel reincarnated," I said.

She turned to me with worry crinkled in her brow. "Do I want to know what that means?"

"Lord of the Rings?" I demanded, more than said. But she still looked blank. I sighed. "Add it to the list." We had a list of movies to watch together and it grew exponentially every week. Apparently befriending a person later in life meant spending most of your time catching up on what came before them. Flo and I could talk forever if we were given the chance.

"But it's like a bazillion hours long!" she protested.

"And worth every one of them," Jesse said, smirking at me. I gave him a nod of appreciation for the support. "Okay." He turned his attention to the coast. "Stand right over here, dear Frodo, and face the water."

Flo shot him a glare. "I might not have seen it but I know who Frodo is."

"It's actually a compliment," I told her. "He has lovely eyes."

"Yeah!" Jesse took Flo's arm and guided her to the lookout point. "The furry feet are inconsequential."

"Are you usually this mean to your models?" Flo said, pouting the way she did to hide her smile.

"Only the hobbits," Jesse replied. He backed up before she could swat him. "Kidding, kidding."

They bickered back and forth for the entirety of the shoot. I wished I could leave them to it, but Flo had insisted I come too. She felt uncomfortable in front of the camera, she claimed—even though it was bound to absolutely love her—and her awkwardness would supposedly be alleviated by my presence.

I was sitting on the sand looking out at the water when I heard his voice. "Do I spot a Dot?"

I spun around to see Darcy, swinging a bag in one hand and his shoes in the other. He was in board shorts the colour of the sky and his hair shone like gold under the sun. A picture of tropical beauty. All he needed was a guitar and a coconut with a straw.

"Hey," I said.

When Darcy arrived anywhere, I couldn't help but smile. And it wasn't just a surface smile, either. The more I'd come to know him, the more it worked its way into me, warming me through.

Darcy and Nina were over. Well and truly. That night we'd seen them hugging was apparently the night of their final goodbyes. Darcy had told Jesse all about it, and now that Jesse and Flo were an item she could pass on most of what he said to me. I knew a lot of things Darcy wouldn't expect me to know. Maybe one day I'd tell him.

He slid to the sand beside me and we hugged– the one-armed kind. Then he turned to Jesse and Flo, who hadn't noticed he'd arrived. Flo was ankle-deep in the water and Jesse was getting a shot from behind.

"Sorry I took so long," he said. "I stopped for supplies."

He pulled a towel out from the bag first and laid it in front of us. Then he took out chips, chocolate, grapes, and bottles of iced tea.

"You've outdone yourself," I told him, plucking at a grape and popping it in my mouth.

"Thanks." He winked at me, so subtly I'd have missed it if I blinked. It was a familiar, conspiratorial gesture he'd only started up recently, and whenever he did it I felt a little closer to him. I supposed it was a small replica of what sharing secrets had the power to do.

"Look at this." Darcy reached for my hat, the corners of his eyes crinkling. "What is this?"

"It's a hat!" I said, soon realising the question was more one of disbelief. Bucket hats were making a comeback. Weren't they? "What's wrong with it?"

Darcy laughed and pulled it down further over my eyes. "Ah, you're so cute."

"I was beginning to think you'd bail," Jesse called. He and Flo were making their way over, Flo in the lead hoisting her dress up off the sand.

"Course not," Darcy said, throwing a bottle of iced tea at Jesse. He fumbled but caught it. Flo dropped hers in the sand and swore. She sat opposite us to wipe it on the towel's edge.

Jesse snapped a photo of us before sinking to the sand beside her. "You know those see-through jelly things that wash up on the shore?" he asked, popping open the chip packet.

"Yeah, yeah." Darcy was nodding. "They're jellyfish skeletons, I've heard. Like, disks of tissue."

"Huh." Jesse crunched on a chip. "Well, once Minty and I came down here, and she tried to eat one. Did I tell you that?"

I wasn't sure who he was asking, but we all shook our heads. He had only started talking about Minty openly in the last couple of weeks, after he finally told Darcy about her.

"What happened?" Flo asked with a faint smile. I could tell she was being careful to keep her voice unaffected by the topic. I'd come to notice that it was one of her countless talents. She could very easily foster a space where you felt comfortable to share even the hardest things.

"I stopped her just in time," Jesse said, staring at the sand like his sister was still there. "She was such a cheeky monkey. Couldn't keep your eyes off her for one second."

Darcy laughed. "So she took after you, then."

Jesse broke out from his reverie to cast him a rueful smile. "Unfortunately."

Half a block of chocolate in, Jesse told us he had an announcement to make. He drum-rolled on an iced tea bottle, and then said, "I got into RMIT."

"*What?*" Flo struck him on the arm, hard. "You didn't even tell me you had the interview!"

Jesse gripped his arm where Flo hit him. "Well I didn't want to make a big deal of it."

"Dude, that's awesome," Darcy said, shoving his shoulder so he fell back onto the sand.

With a long-suffering sigh, Jesse pressed himself back up. Then he raised his brows at me in question. "Do you want to hit me too?"

"Maybe," I said. "Congrats, though. That's really exciting."

"I thought *this* shoot was for your portfolio," Flo said.

"Oh, nah." Jesse smirked across at her. "This was just for fun." That earned him another whack.

———◆———

Once the chocolate and chips were demolished, Darcy got to his feet and stripped off his tee shirt. He was lean and tanned underneath it. I was allowing myself a second or two to observe this fact when he turned to me, held out his hand and said, "Come on, bucket head."

I took it but shook my bucket head. "I didn't bring bathers." He pulled and I resisted, which conveniently allowed our hands to stay linked a little longer.

"Don't need them—it's like thirty degrees," Darcy said. "You'll dry off in five seconds."

I didn't love the idea of getting my dress and underwear wet, but he was convincing enough.

"Fine." I let Darcy drag me up, expecting him to let go. But he didn't. He held my hand loosely in his all the way to the water. It felt highly conspicuous, particularly with two sets of prying eyes behind us. I tried not to think about them, though.

It was no secret to Flo that I liked the guy—and therefore probably no secret to Jesse either.

"The beach was one of the first places I came after my … hibernation," I told him. "Emma and Flo took me down to Elwood."

Darcy's thumb skirted my palm and a shiver ran through me. If he noticed, I hoped he'd attribute it to the icy water lapping at my thighs. Why was it so cold in thirty-degree heat? Ah Melbourne, our fickle friend.

"How was it?" Darcy asked. I was learning that he was rarely direct, and occasionally that was irritating, but mostly it was lovely. He asked thoughtful questions–questions you could take a number of ways, like he had left the directions open for you to choose which one to take.

"It was nice," I answered. Darcy let the silence hang, so I decided to fill it with more. "I guess, the ocean is big and scary just like the world is, but the water covers it all up like a blanket. So you don't see the really scary things. You just get the shells and the treasures that wash up from it."

Darcy ran his thumb across my hand again, then squeezed it tighter. "You mean–it's easier to face."

"Kind of." I felt a bit silly trying to articulate it. "But all the bad stuff exists anyway, whether we see it or we don't. Staying cooped up forever would be like staring at the water without stepping into it, or sitting on the sand without looking for shells. Know what I mean?"

He didn't answer right away, which caused my whole body to stiffen. Had I opened the inner sanctum of my mind a little too much for his comfort? I bit down on my lip and waited.

Darcy was frowning, looking down at our feet. I wished I knew what he was thinking. He tugged on my hand and I let him pull me deeper, let my dress meet the water, my hips, my chest.

I hoped he was right about drying off fast. I didn't want to soak into Jesse's car seats the rest of the way home.

That worry soon vanished because only our heads were above water now and Darcy was holding my waist. His fingers dug into me a little as a wave swept our feet off the sand and brought them back again. Then I saw his eyes flicker to the beach behind me. Was he checking on Jesse and Flo? Or was he about to suggest we go back? Maybe he thought my beach analogy was lame. Maybe it was.

But then his gaze returned. He flipped up the front of my bucket hat and kissed me.

With the rush of another wave, our bodies met. My hands lifted to his neck and I held on tight. His lips were salty and smooth and they found mine urgently each time we came together.

Another few waves shifted us nearer to shore until we weren't lifted off our feet anymore. We stood with our toes in the sand and the kiss turned slow. Gentle.

I never wanted it to end. I'd found a treasure. Ironically, a treasure I had discovered in the ocean itself. Maybe my beach analogy wasn't so lame after all—because even amidst the widest expanse of the strange and unknown, there was something here worth braving it for.

Closed

The mark on my neck had almost disappeared. I touched the faint line, peering at it under the pale light above the bathroom mirror. I remembered it still—vividly. The feeling of the blade against my throat. If I shut my eyes and thought back to that night, it was as real as ever. But I was able to remember, and that was important. Some people didn't have the privilege.

I brushed my teeth and went back to my room, where Kramer was already spread at the base of my bed.

It was funny, how what felt trivial once could suddenly become vital. How the light could outshine the dark. I paused with my finger on the switch of my lamp, taking a moment to look across at Flo's *Corner* painting.

There would always be the dark side, as she'd drawn it. But as all-consuming as it might have felt, it was never all there was.

Sure, the black was flat. A wide nothingness where you were made to feel empty. A place where nothing mattered except fear, and everything to do with friendships or boys or family seemed meaningless beside it.

But just a step away, there was colour.

Nothing was trivial in the colour. Every stroke mattered. The black consumed, but the colour could too. A shell on the shore, a backyard picnic, truth confided under fairy lights, milkshakes on a seesaw, a boy on a beach.

Little pictures of infinity.

Acknowledgements

This book is for the people that brought it together. I want to begin by thanking three beautiful souls whose lives I was lucky enough to intersect with three years ago.

Dearest Julia–you are warmth, spontaneity and readiness to listen. You are the person that unites. ('The glue.') Your company is infectious, and your ability to discuss everything under the sun without a speck of judgment makes speaking with you a joy, always. Thank you for the countless conversations we've shared that have shaped this story, and for your consistent excitement about it, right back when it was only a seed. Your insights during the editing process were instrumental in rounding this story in all the right places.

Dearest Xanthe–you are calmness, intelligence and strength. You never fail to reach an insightful conclusion, way before I get there. I'm constantly amazed by the way you carry yourself. I will never forget the moment I felt like I might crumble and you took my shoulders, looked me in the eye and breathed with me until I was able to bear it. You channel strength, even when your own is being tested. It's a gift, and I love you for it.

Dearest Clancy–you are honesty, compassion and fire. You remember the little things, the important things. You *notice*. I don't think you realise how much this has helped me along the last few years. To feel cared for and loved and listened to–it alters you from the inside out. It makes me want to be more *me* because I know there's someone there, wanting to see the truest version.

I can't imagine my life without any one of you.

A million thanks to my grandmother and precious mother for your careful and thoughtful edits. Your grammar checks, opinions and understanding of this story's purpose are invaluable, as are you.

Thank you to my wider TGIF family. My unwavering tribe. To the stream of faces that whirl around in my memories of the restaurant–the ones who taught me the ropes, rushed to help when I dropped glasses, argued about who would clean the dishwasher, dug into leftover birthday cakes, sung birthday songs when I couldn't muster the courage, made Oreo shakes without asking, stayed for close even after clocking off, went for pancakes at all hours, and made every moment in that place a privilege.

And to Alex–you are the reason I'm writing this at all. Thank you for your energy, your art, your passion and your wit. Although you aren't here with us, so much of you lasts. I'm reluctant to call this a tribute, because your real tribute isn't bound to fiction.

It's what we all remember and will never forget. It's that piece of you that each one of us will take around every corner for the rest of our lives.

About the Author

HAYLEY GABRIELLE is a Melbourne-based writer of poetry, fantasy and young adult fiction. She has seen works published across a range of journals and anthologies worldwide, has claimed a place in the AMP Tomorrow Maker program, and won the 2018 Alan Marshall Short Story Award. Hayley's venture into longer works of fiction began with *The Essence Chronicles*, followed by *Corner*, a standalone novel.

To keep up to date with Hayley's latest releases, subscribe at
www.hayleygabrielle.com

or check out @hayleygabriellewriter on Instagram to follow Hayley's writing journey.

www.ingramcontent.com/pod-product-compliance
Lightning Source LLC
Chambersburg PA
CBHW021408110726
47901CB00008B/2103